An Anjie Vilekar Investigation

her quest to avenge the girl in the long grass

P V Pradhan

Copyright © 2024 P V Pradhan

Los Angeles, California

Library of Congress Control Number: 2024922602

Cover designed by Get covers

ISBN-978-1-965408-69-8

DEDICATION

To,
My parents, who instilled in us that hard work was
the only way to achieve anything meaningful.

.

DEDICATION

To,
My parents, who instilled in us that hard work was
the only way to achieve anything meaningful.

Contents

Prologue.. 1

Chapter I 3

Chapter II 10

Chapter III 30

Chapter IV 43

Chapter V.. 47

Chapter VI 64

Chapter VII 67

Chapter VIII 73

Chapter IX 90

Chapter X.. 97

Chapter XI 115

Chapter XII 119

Chapter XIII 127

Chapter XIV 146

Chapter XV 152

Chapter XVI... 164

Chapter XVII.. 175

Chapter XVIII 189

Chapter XIX 202

Chapter XX 205

Chapter XXI 223

Chapter XXII 240

Chapter XXIII 254

Chapter XXIV 293

Chapter XXV 312

Chapter XXVI 326

Chapter XXVII 349

Epilogue 372

ALSO BY THE AUTHOR 375

Prologue

The paramedics were onto the scene less than five minutes after the 911 call came in. They were battle hardened, these paramedics. And experienced.

Yet they could do nothing. It was too late. And the age of the victim was no surprise. No surprise but sad, nonetheless.

Another young man, barely in his twenties, the victim of an overdose. Who knew what the lethal combination was this time. There were all sorts of permutations and combinations on the market.

The paramedics declared the victim dead on arrival. The time and place of death were duly noted. The police officers on the scene watched silently as the ambulance pulled away.

The coroner's report would decide whether to launch a criminal investigation. But, at the moment, it looked like just another senseless tragedy.

Chapter I

Jay

I think I have seen maybe one car pass us by in the last mile or so. We haven't been able to keep our hands off each other since we started. My hand is inside her blouse, caressing her back, making her giggle. L is stroking my face with the back of her hand from time to time. We are in her red Corvette. And when we turn on the dirt road, I know we are going to have the place to ourselves. Even so, the location is a bit of a surprise.

'Fuck, L, I didn't know we were coming here,' I say to L, some surprise evident in my voice.

L turns to face me.

'I said somewhere nice and quiet,' she says, with a smile.

One thing I know, there's no point in arguing with L. If she has made up her mind, it will take a lot to make her change it. Moreover, for me, this is definitely not a hill to die on. We drive about half a mile on the dirt road until we come to a small, unpaved, parking area. This is Colver Park, a nature park, mainly trees, long grass and shrubbery, that is popular with local residents for bird-watching and walking. The hikers, cross-country runners and bikers usually go to Swope Park, which closes at twelve am. Here in Colver Park, there are a couple of mini fields where the kids play soccer or just throw footballs around. Many a soccer ball has been lost in the seeming wilderness. And no one is likely bird-watching at this hour, not in this wilderness.

Lise-Anne parks the car and looks at me.

'You ready?' she asks.

Lise-Anne, or L as I call her, is the star point guard on our college basketball team. I watch her every game, not because I am a stalker or a crazed fan, but because I am in the cheerleading squad. We have one of the best women's basketball teams in our league and L is the star. If we ever have a long relationship, she is the one who will likely bring in the moolah. But that's too far out. We've never even made out; well, not at any length. This is the first time we've planned to have a session. You see, L's boyfriend is on the swim team. And while things have not been going so swimmingly well with them, she's not ready yet to call it a day. So, you can say I'm an interview for the rebound. But I don't care.

So, I answer - Yes.

Beyond the parking lot there is the tall grass, trees and shrubs, with some open ground thrown in, not to mention the trails that are quite popular. We both know this place well. Moreover, we are both avid hunters and used to the quiet of the woods.

L grabs a blanket and a flashlight and turns to me,

'Get the Glock from the glove box. Be careful, it's loaded.'

I open the glove box and get the gun. It's a Glock 43, nice and compact, exactly the kind I would expect L to carry. I shove the gun in my waistband and we enter the woods. L knows this place well. After walking around fifty yards, we come to a clearing in the tall grass. It's a nice place, really beautiful, in the stillness of the night and the moonlight shining down. And beautiful Lise-Anne, right in front of me.

We start with kisses, slow kisses that get more passionate and urgent. L pulls away and looks at me.

'Well, get started,' she says.

And yet, when the moment arrives, I feel a slight trepidation. I feel like I'm unable to take the next step.

'You can touch me, I'm not gonna bite,' L says, her eyes looking into mine.

My heart is pounding in my chest as I step toward her. I think we both gasp when I reach for the first button of her blouse and my hand touches her skin. Slowly, taking my time, I unbutton her blouse – one button at a time. I want to take in every moment. By the time I'm done with the last, I am fairly sure I'm out of breath. Her leggings come off faster because my now the urgency is building. And then, suddenly, L is right in front of me, all of her, and whatever I had pictured in my mind doesn't even come close. Her skin is glowing in the moonlight, her wavy hair is draped behind her shoulders.

My turn now. First, I set the gun down and then we both proceed with the rest of my *vêtements*. She appears to be a bit impatient with the progress and pulls off the one sock left, which she flings away.

I don't have time to protest. Our mouths are locked immediately. I really consider myself, at this time and place, to be the luckiest guy in the world. We have been waiting for this moment for a long, long time and now that it's here, we are not going to waste it. We take our time, though, exploring each other. Our hands and mouths are all over each other. I reach L's deepest recesses and she moans. I am convinced that point guards make the best lovers. I have completely lost track of time. Our lovemaking builds up and up and finally reaches a crescendo.

'Jay, oh god, Jay,' she screams out, digging her fingers into my skin.

'L,' I say, 'L,' when I reach my moment, right alongside her.

Exhausted, we lie side by side, only the sound of our breaths breaking the silence.

Le petit mort, the French have such an elegant way of putting these things. Even the stars seem to have turned a brighter shade of electric blue.

After a few moments, L rolls on her side toward me and kisses me.

'Omg, Jay, that was amazing. We have to do this again.'

I kiss her back. She really is so beautiful; I could kiss her all day and night.

'L, you are the most beautiful girl I've ever seen,' I tell her.

We start making out again, but in the middle of it, L looks at her watch.

'I gotta go, Jay. It's a noon game. If coach finds out I broke curfew, she'll put me on the bench for sure.'

I nod in understanding. Reluctantly, we start to get dressed. I can't help looking at her. When she asks me to help with her clasp, my heart skips a beat. She laughs.

'Are you going to keep looking at me or get your clothes on?' she asks.

'What do you think?' I answer and L giggles.

Finally, I get dressed and put the gun back in the waistband. The only thing remaining is the errant sock. I've forgotten where L threw it.

'Where do you think it is,' I ask.

'Forget the sock,' she says.

'Just feels weird,' I point out.

L thinks for a moment and points in a general direction further out.

I set off in the direction and walk a few yards. I sweep the area with the flashlight. At the outer edge of my sweep, I suddenly notice the glint of an eye. A single eye. My heart starts beating faster.

'There's something here looking at me,' I yell out to L as I grip the gun and pull it out of my waistband.

I step forward toward the glint; real small, slow steps, ready to fire. I sweep aside the grass and point the gun at the object.

It's a woman's purse, with a glinting rhinestone. I pick it up and sweep the flashlight further out to check for any other objects, my sock among them.

A few steps further, I turn around and yell.

'We gotta get the fuck outta here, fast!!'

Chapter II

Anjie (Anjali) Vilekar, Detective – Homicide, Kansas City, Missouri PD

My bedroom

I am in the middle of my sleep when I hear the phone. I think it must be REM sleep because I feel like the ringing is part of my dream. It takes me a couple of seconds before I realize it's my real-world cell. For a moment, I wonder who it could be. I hope it's not my parents, that's one of my worst fears: mom or dad calling at this hour. It cannot be Rohan; he's sleeping right next to me. I narrow it down to one: Detective John Roman, my senior partner in the Kansas City Homicide division. Roman is the detective on call. Any homicide reported off-hours will be dispatched to him.

Rohan's arm is draped across me. The phone ringing doesn't seem to have had any effect on his sleep at all. I must say I envy that ability. I gently remove his hand

and place it on his side, roll over to the nightstand on my left and pick up the phone, trying to get my bearings at the same time.

'Vilekar, we have a db [dead body] in Colver Park, how soon can you get there?' John's crisp voice comes over the phone.

'I can be there in twenty minutes,' I answer.

'Good, I'm on my way. See you there,' he hangs up.

Colver Park is around fifteen minutes from my place. I've given myself five minutes to get ready. The lights and siren will clear whatever traffic there is at this hour.

I exit my apartment in just under three minutes. Rohan is half-awake when I leave.

'Duty calls,' I tell him.

'Ok, babe,' he murmurs and goes back to sleep.

When I arrive in the parking area, I see three marked vehicles already there, lights flashing. I park my car and walk up to the officers. I see Roman talking to one of them. His car is parked a little further out.

'Vilekar, I was just talking about cordoning off the area. The db is a bit further out.'

'When are the lab techs arriving?' I ask.

'They should be here shortly. Meanwhile, I've asked for a couple of floodlights to cover the scene,' Roman informs me.

'Do we have ID yet?'

'The first to respond went through her purse for ID. Name is Tina Adams, age twenty-five. Address is an apartment building about ten minutes from here.'

I am struck by the age. Tina's age is right around where I am. A full life to live. Whatever happened that it has been struck down so abruptly? That's my job to find out.

'Are we securing the apartment?' I inquire.

'I've asked dispatch to send a unit to check if anyone is there. If its empty, we'll put a seal until we get a search warrant,' Roman answers.

'Who called it in?'

'Couple of college kids. A romp in the moonlight. They hightailed it out and called 911. My guess is they won't be visiting this place in a hurry.'

The police officers are setting up the crime scene tape as we walk down to the area that is now lit up by floodlights. I guess it to be around seventy-five yards or so from the parking area. We walk through the tall grass, looking at the ground all the time, keeping a watch for any objects or markings. The whole area is a crime scene and everything in it is potentially evidence.

I have my shoe protectors on to avoid contaminating the scene. We approach the floodlit area, located a little further away from a clearing. Tina Adams is a young woman, looking younger than the age listed on her driver's license. Her blonde hair is well-coiffed, a little shorter than shoulder length. Her clothes are simple but seem to be good quality. A yellow short-sleeve shirt, a pair of capri pants and pumps. Nothing unusual. Her left hand is by her side while the right one is across her stomach. At first glance, this does not look to me the scene of the shooting. It's not clear whether it was deliberately placed in such a manner or that happened while placing her on the ground. The watch on her left hand is a ladies-model Cartier. The most obvious thing I notice is the bullet hole in her torso, her yellow shirt stained red around the area. Tina has already been examined by the patrol officer, but for my own satisfaction I need to make sure. I reach down and feel her pulse. There is none. Next, I remove a small mirror from my jacket pocket and hold it against her nose. There is no vapor.

'Confirmed that Tina Adams has passed away,' I say to Roman.

Roman nods.

'Cod [cause of death] would seem to be a single GSW [gunshot wound] to the torso. The caliber likely 9mm. No other sign of bruising or struggle. No sign of sexual assault, at least not from the state of the clothing,' I add.

The bullet wound is on the upper left side of the torso. I lift her gently to look at the underside of the wound.

'it's a through and through. The exit wound is parallel to the entry,' I call out.

'She was shot standing up,' Roman surmises.

Roman is following my progress, taking notes in his spiral notebook. We will share and compare our notes later. He walks around the body. It is surrounded by grass, making it very difficult to see clearly in the dark. On the other side of Tina, the tall grass looks like it has been mowed down in a broad swath.

Roman looks at me.

'The killer drove the vehicle to this spot. It was too far and too risky to drag her all the way. Easier to get the car to the spot, take a look around and dump the body,' I give my analysis.

Roman nods.

'That's how I read it. We have an approximate timeline with the 911 callers. They arrived around one am and made the call around one forty-five am. The body was dumped sometime before they entered the premises, that's for sure. We'll need to get a tod [time of death] and trace her movements.'

We move to the spot where the purse is located. It's not very far from the body.

'The male caller picked it up, but put it down once he saw the body. According to him, it's very close to its original position,' Roman informs me.

'Looks like it was flung. I don't see any reason why it would be deliberately placed a few yards away,' I observe.

'I agree,' says Roman.

I mark the spot where the purse is located and then take some photographs from different angles. I then pick it up with my gloved hands and gently open it.

Inside, there are pretty much items that you would expect in a woman's purse: lipstick, credit cards, cell phone and a key that looks like an apartment key. The driver's license is there, as well, with the name and address that the patrol officers saw. I look over at Roman.

'I don't see anything special here. No car key. We will need to go through the credit cards and contacts.'

He nods in agreement. I place the purse in an evidence bag that I will later hand over to forensics.

'We can do a canvass of the immediate vicinity now but a full canvass would be better done in daylight. I checked Google Earth; there are no bodies of water nearby. The nearest lake is half a mile away,' I suggest to Roman. Bodies of water are usually popular places to ditch murder weapons.

'We'll see if we have sufficient reason to believe the weapon was disposed of in the lake. I'm also going to ask forensics to check if they can identify the type of vehicle used,' Roman answers.

'We will need to brief Elsworth before we go to her apartment,' I add.

Marci Elsworth is the Lieutenant we report to.

'That's what I was thinking too. Let's grab a quick shut-eye and a bite and regroup at the station first thing. We may have some background on the victim by that time, I hope. We need to notify the next of kin before making any details public,' Roman gives a plan of action.

The morning has now taken over from the night. I enter my apartment and wonder if it's worth crawling back into bed. Rohan has already left. I decide against more sleep and choose a shower instead. After a hot shower and a cup of fresh, black coffee, I feel more energy than I would with a nap.

I'm going through the photographs and case notes when my phone rings. Roman.

'We have located the next of kin. I would like to notify them right away. You want to join me?'

'Sure, give me the address. I'll meet you there.'

Jacob Adams's residence

The drive is almost an hour. After getting off the highway, I get on a dirt road for a couple of miles before coming to a long-winded driveway ending in what looks to be a huge farmhouse. The single-story structure is prominent in the midst of a field. Two barn-like buildings are on either side. The driveway is not paved but rather a mix of fine and coarse river rocks. It adds to the rural aura, seemingly a world away from the concrete jungle of the city. I have coordinated with Roman so that we arrive together. I have parked my car outside the property. Two cars would appear unnecessarily intimidating.

We walk up to the house and Roman raps his knuckles a couple of times.

The door is opened by a young man, who appears to be in his mid-thirties.

'Mr. Jacob Adams?' I inquire.

The young man nods. He is Tina's older brother. He has been expecting us but does not know the tragic reason why.

'I'm Det. Vilekar and this is Det. Roman, of the Kansas City police,' I make the introductions.

Informing family members of the death of a loved one is perhaps the most painful duty there is. There is no sugar-coating the news and try as we might to be sympathetic, that moment of sorrow is unique.

Jacob asks us if we are sure and we show the driver's license and a photograph of Tina's face. He confirms the identity. I do not want to describe his grief. There are no words. He will come down to the morgue to identify his sister personally.

At some point in the very near future, we will need to talk with Jacob and perhaps other family members. But this is not the time.

We walk back to our car..

Tina Adams's apartment, KC

Elsworth looks up as I enter her office, followed by Roman. She is in the midst of going through reports on her computer. Captain Frank Wright is seated in one of the rather plush chairs.

'I take it you have informed Tina's brother,' she says, more a statement than a question.

Roman nods in agreement.

'He was the one who opened the door,' I inform her.

'I just got some reports about the victim and her family background. Looks like they are a pretty well-known family in business circles. They deal with farm equipment; sales and leasing. That's pretty big in the

Midwest. Well to do, obviously. Started by Jacob's grandfather and then passed down to his son. Now it fallen to Jacob. I'm not sure what role Tina was playing in running the business, if any. We should have some more details soon,' Elsworth shares the information with us.

'Jacob is coming by later for identification. We hope to get an interview with the family if possible. It might help with motive,' Roman adds.

'Well, be careful and prepare well. Jacob Adams is a big player in these parts. Be sure to do your homework before you ask any questions,' Elsworth cautions us.

'Jacob Adams has also been a regular sponsor of police events and children's activities over the last few years,' Wright adds, to make sure we get the complete picture.

'Jacob is not a suspect at this stage. It's not a statement, we want to get a better idea of the victim's life,' I say, I think rather defensively.

'Well, I am pushing the lab and the IT guys to get you the information as quickly as possible. We'll try to get the autopsy done quickly as well to release the body to the family,' Elsworth says, reassuringly.

'We're going to go over to Tina's place. The landlord has informed us she was the sole tenant. We already have the warrant, just to cover our bases,' Roman informs the bosses.

Both Elsworth and Wright nod in agreement; Roman and I get up to leave.

Tina's apartment is in a three-story building, just around four miles from Colver Park. The building architecture is modern, metal and glass being the look from the outside. I park the car, Roman is riding with me. A patrol car is parked on the street.

Roman and I walk up to the patrol car. The patrolman sees us and nods in acknowledgment.

'All clear then?' I ask.

'All secured. My partner is up there,' he replies.

The address on the driver's license is listed as Apartment 512. Roman punches in the code that we have received from the landlord. The door buzzes open and we step inside.

We take the elevator to the fifth floor. The apartment is easily identifiable by the presence of police tape. We duck under the tape and step inside. It's a small apartment, what one could call a starter for a young professional. It is neatly kept with good décor, giving an impression that the person living here had good taste and took care of the place.

The apartment does not look to be the crime scene. Everything is too well organized. I look around and what catches my eye are the books in the apartment. Almost all the books are related to law. I see some with titles related to Corporate Finance, Mergers, Special Purpose Acquisition Companies and the like. I also spot a few related to drug laws, the penal code and rules of evidence.

On one of the tables is a folder with the imprimatur of Gilchrist College, School of Law.

'Looks like Tina was studying law at Gilchrist,' I remark to Roman, pointing to the folder with the college name on it.

He looks over and nods.

'Excellent school they have over there.'

Gilchrist College is a selective college that offers programs in liberal arts. Their School of Law is consistently ranked among the top in the country. The tuition is up there as well. Despite the cost, the number of applicants keeps climbing each year.

I open a filing cabinet with hanging folders located in a corner of the room. One of the folders is marked from a firm I recognize.

'Some official documents from Lambert & Burnham,' I point out.

Lambert & Burnham is a well-known law firm with offices in downtown Kansas City.

'If she was still a student, then probably an intern or part-time, balancing that with her studies,' Roman surmises.

The bedroom is furnished with a twin-size bed. A small table and a compact chair are beside the bed. On the table is a laptop, closed down, along with some loose papers, which at first glance look to be study materials. The laptop is taken into evidence. As are the papers that have been found in the search.

After the apartment examination is done, Roman and I drive to the crime scene where we were early this morning. The canvass is almost wrapped up. Nothing new has been discovered. All the same, the lab photographers have taken new photos in daylight. They assure us that the pictures will be sent to us by end of day.

'So, first impressions, how do you think this played out?' I ask Roman.

'As far as the body is concerned, I think the unsub [unknown subject of an investigation] was probably in the vicinity somewhere before the drop. Highly unlikely Tina was shot here. Too risky. So, he loads her in his car or truck and probably stakes out a position nearby, waiting for an opportunity. How long that was will be clearer after we get the tod. Then he quickly drives on to the grass and dumps the body and takes off. We will need to recreate the sequence of events going further back once we get more information.'

'If Tina was a student at Gilchrist and then working at Lambert & Burnham, we may get some idea about her whereabouts during the day. We can build up from there. I'm going to set up appointments with the college and the law firm. We can probably cross-reference her phone and email contacts with her colleagues to see who was communicating with,' I give my reading.

Roman nods.

'Her personal life, her professional life. It could be a DV [domestic violence incident] for all we know,' Roman adds.

'We've got an APB out for her car as well. It wasn't at her apartment. That may give us a better direction in tracing her movements.'

'I will be in and out of court over the next few days. The Jeremy Lloyd case. Just a heads-up,' Roman informs me.

The Jeremy Lloyd case involves a police-involved shooting and subsequent arrest of the accused. He is being tried on charges of drug possession and attempt to murder a law enforcement officer. It's a potential life sentence case.

'I'll carry on and keep you informed. Let me know when you are testifying, I'll be there for support.'

'Will do. I will be meeting the DA soon to go over what they will be covering. In the meantime, let's set up those appointments and push the lab guys.'

Scene of the crime

I'm at my desk, in the middle of writing my report on the search when I see the message – Tina's SUV has been found in a location around 3 miles from Colver Park. Considering the fact that Tina was already dead when her body was dumped in the park, the SUV could well be the crime scene. I quickly call back to make sure that the officers do not interfere with the vehicle, beyond ensuring their safety.

I call forensics to get the techs out there stat.

John and I reach there as quick as we can, the lights and sirens clearing us a path. The SUV is standing beside a dirt road bordering a lake. It's a Chevy Trailblazer. We already had that description from the DMV.

This location is not too far from Colver Park. That makes sense; the killer not wanting to transport the body over a long distance.

'Has anyone touched the interior?' John asks.

'No. I just opened the doors to make sure there was no imminent threat. Had my gloves on,' the officer answers.

John nods. I open the front driver-side door and then the rear passenger door to check if any objects have been left behind. There is nothing except for a box of tissue on the back seat. I take pictures with my cell phone. Forensics will take their own photos as well.

I then open the rear hatch. There I see a gym bag, with a logo of one of the popular KC gyms. But, clearly visible, are also dried blood streaks, including a place where the blood has pooled, the location may very likely match the wound made by the bullet.

I turn to John.

'It's looks like Tina's body was dumped from her own SUV. And the bullet was a through and through. The blood is hers,' I reason.

'If the tire tracks match, then we've lost a lead. So, this is where the car was kept. The perp carries out the murder, uses the vic's own car to dump the body. Then doubles back here and gets away in their own vehicle,' John draws out the likely scenario.

'That makes this location the scene of the crime. We'll need to look around for a bullet. It shouldn't go that far once it goes through the body. I'll ask for a canvassing with metal detectors.'

I look around the area for signs of a struggle. Since it's a dirt road, any struggle would maybe result in some scuff marks on the ground or some other sign of disturbance in the shrubbery. I don't find any. That's not conclusive, of course. It's likely the murder was committed somewhere else and there was a struggle over there, but Occam's Razor is very useful as a tool.

'If there is no blood on the driver's seat or thereabouts, the perp is probably not injured, at least not seriously,' John hypothesizes.

I am in agreement.

John and I carry out a canvass of the scene, covering a fifty-yard radius, looking mainly for the bullet. It's not to be found, however.

Once we are done with the scene, forensics takes over. I talk to the team lead and he assures me that they will have a report on the blood by the next day.

'It's a bit of a lucky break. If the car had been scuttled in the lake, that would make our job much harder,' I remark to John.

'The silver lining,' he adds.

The luck has carried a bit further. Within two hours, I get a message that the bullet was found lodged in a tree. It's been sent to the lab for analysis. I call Hansie, my contact at the lab to try and see if we can put this on a high priority.

This also confirms that the location where Tina's SUV was found is the scene of the crime. Another piece of the puzzle that lies before us.

Chapter III

Anjie

McBurnie's

McBurnie's is a popular bar. Although it is not exclusively a cop bar, there are usually a few of my colleagues here, given that the location is not too far from the precinct.

I look around as I carry my beer and nachos to a table surrounded by three chairs. There's a popular song playing, from the 00's. Not that I'm complaining. I still love it when I hear Feliz Navidad during the holiday season. Great music is great music; it stands the test of time.

I'm feeling a little out of place here, much as I usually do amongst a crowd. It's the whole South Asian Female Detective thing. I mean, the job is hard enough without having to live up to another set of expectations, setting a standard for the community. It's not the path that my parents had envisioned for me, growing up. But then, I've rarely done what they expected, sometimes surprising myself along the way. Take my choice of sport, as an example. My parents had enrolled me in Gymnastics. I was pretty good. My parents are big gymnastics fans. Simone Biles is their absolute favorite. But somewhere during middle school, I started playing volleyball; playing with a bunch of friends in my backyard. It helped that there were some who were pretty good. I took a liking and I got pretty good at it. My parents hadn't really given much thought to volleyball. Their dream was that I would represent the country, in gymnastics, at the Olympics and help the team win the gold medal. So, volleyball was not on their radar. I think they were surprised that I was selected on the college team and even more surprised that I won the 'Best Setter' award at the inter-collegiate tournament. Like I said, I am good at it. I think I like the mind games within the sport, especially for the position I play. Nothing like the satisfaction of setting up a good, clean spike.

But what really surprised my family, even my friends, was my deciding to join the police. My mother had implored me to reconsider.

'How's this as compared to becoming a doctor or lawyer? How far are you going to go?' she had asked.

I didn't really have an answer then. The glass ceiling is a reality for people of color. That is a hard fact. But I had noticed that, among law enforcement, there was a genuine push to recruit from the community so that the force reflected the diversity. So, while I didn't have a ready answer for my mother, I replied best I could.

'I really believe that if I work hard and do well in what I am supposed to, I can reach as high as anyone.' It was an answer from the heart.

She had not been convinced. But she also realized that there was very little she could do. In the end, mother wanted me to be happy and successful, in that order.

My parents are generally supportive of my decisions. Take my boyfriend in high school. Ken was my classmate in my junior year and we were friends before we started dating. The first time I brought him home, I was really quite anxious about my parents' reaction. They, however, could not have been more welcoming.

'If you are going out with someone, we want to know that person.

And we want to know that he is kind and considerate toward you,' my father had explained.

It has never been in my nature to keep secrets, least of all from my parents. At the end of the day, I know they are on my side. That's all that matters.

Funny thing about Ken is that I was equally anxious when my mom made *pakoras* as a snack. I was so worried that he will find it too spicy, too ethnic, but I was so happy so see that he enjoyed it. I then found out he was a big fan of Indian food. So much so, I began to wonder if he was dating me for the food.

My parents and younger brother have always called me 'Anju'. However, in pre-school, somehow, Anjali was shortened to Anjie. I sometimes call myself Anjie as well, especially in the Starbucks queue and even on emails with friends. To be true to the original, I have kept the 'j'. Many of my close friends call me by my shortened name, but in the KCPD, its usually the last name, except for some close friends. My partner,

Roman, always refers to me as Vilekar. That's fine and great and the way I prefer it.

I am biting down on a tortilla chip when, out of the corner of my eye, I spot a familiar figure approaching.

'Anjie,' Det. Jordan Burns calls out, as she flashes her brilliant smile. She is one of my closest friends on the department.

'Jordie,' I smile back, as we give each other a hug.

'I see you started already,' she says, with a slight mocking roll of her eyes.

'I was both thirsty and hungry,' I reply, with a smile, Jordan pours herself a beer and raises her glass.

'Cheers,' we say, clinking our glasses. I must say, the nice cold beer feels so great at the end of a hard day.

'Your team in the playoffs again?' she asks.

I play in a competitive volleyball league. Sometimes, I think that is the only thing that keeps me from obsessing over what I see in my job.

'We are in the second round. I think we can mount a serious challenge for the title this time.'

'How's the Adams case going?' Jordan inquires. The case has been the talk of the precinct.

'Gotten started, we're trying to trace the movements of the vic, trying to line up some of her college and workplace colleagues. Once we get the tod, we'll know what kind of timeframe we're working with.'

'What was her age, I heard twenty-five?'

'Yeah, she reminded me of me, and you. Young lady, probably figuring out her life. That's the worst part, right? I guess speaking and acting on their behalf is the best you can do,' I shake my head, thinking about the young woman, lying in the grass.

'That's the job,' Jordan adds.

The band is playing some lively country tunes and an impromptu line dance has broken out. I'm half tempted to join.

A young man is passing by our table and nods to us. Then he seems to think of something and turns toward me.

'You look familiar,' he addresses me.

'Is that the best you got?' I look at him quizzically.

'No, no, not a pickup line. I think I've seen you on TV. On a cop show, I think,' he seems to be working hard, trying to scratch his memory.

'Let me guess, you just saw that new Bollywood movie.'

'Yeah, that's it,' he exclaims, before realizing his mistake.

'So, to you, we all look alike, huh?' I ask, before bursting into laughter seeing the look on his face.

'Sorry, my bad,' he says.

'Don't worry, you're not the first guy to think I'm Sunita,' I smile at him. He seems like a nice young man.

'Cute guy,' Jordan remarks, after he's left our table.

'That he is. Too bad, though, that I'm not getting Sunita's salary. I reckon I could retire after one year and spend the rest of my life on a beach in Spain.'

'I think you can still do that, given your family fortune. Isn't your dad's company worth like a billion dollars?' Jordan points out.

'Three-hundred-fifty million, Jordie. And that's if I join my dad's business or become a doctor and join my mom. Either way, I'm not doing what I want to. I don't want to spend my life that way,' I explain the logic that I've played in my mind umpteen number of times.

Jordan sighs and shakes her head.

'Choices,' she says and I nod.

We decide to join the line dance. All the laughter and the enthusiasm make me forget about the events of the recent past for a short while. I think I'm a good dancer, but Jordan is really good. There a couple of songs later, we return to our table, thirstier.

'You got the moves, girl,' Jordan says to me, giving me a high-five.

'You looked so great out there,' I give her my honest opinion.

'Don't look now, Josh is coming by,' Jordan gives me a heads-up.

Josh Myers, rookie, is indeed enroute and stops by our table.

'Good evening, lovely ladies,' he greets us.

We both smile back. Josh is a really great guy and a bit of a precinct heartthrob. Today, he has two tickets to the next Chiefs home game and is looking for a partner. Everyone in KC is a Chiefs fan.

I'm planning to spend some time with my younger brother. Jordan is pretty occupied, she says. Josh spends a few minutes with us and moves on. I don't think he will have trouble finding someone to go with him. The seats are pretty good as well, around the 50-yard line.

Jordan and I are later joined by some of our colleagues. Like I said, it's a bar that's popular with cops. I decide to call it a day and head back to my apartment.

Its late in the evening. I let myself in and head to my bedroom. On the way I see my roommate, Mei, fixing herself a meal, while simultaneously carrying on a conversation on her cell, which is lodged between her shoulders and face. I find this multi-tasking to be more complex than it appears.

I change into casuals, shorts and halter top, and open my department laptop.

There is an email from the lab. There is a preliminary report on the bullet. It's a 9 mm. There is no further information on whether there was a hit on the databases. I think it unlikely that there will be a hit, but there is always a chance. A 9mm by itself doesn't help us much. It's the most popular caliber there is, almost every household having one and often more handguns with that ammunition.

Nowadays, with the backlog, mainly due to staffing shortages, databases checks take longer and longer. An IBIS check may take two or three days, in-state checks may take just as long or longer and out-of-state checks can take a real long time. No use complaining about it, that's just the way things are right now.

The crime scene photos are on a secured, encrypted folder on the police cloud. I go through the photos that were taken when we first arrived on the scene and compare them to those taken in daylight. The body, of course, had been removed from the scene before the sun had come up. On close examination, there looked to be nothing that had been missed. The flattened grass was more obvious in the daytime photos. The vehicle used by the unsub looked to have been driven from the parking area to the disposal site, a short distance away, then backed up before leaving the scene. Tire impressions were not clearly visible and because the vehicle had driven and backed up over the same patch of grass, it wouldn't be easy to discern the tire size. But the techs in the lab could probably give an opinion.

In the early stages of an investigation, there is always a temptation to form theories and conjectures.

Sometimes you become fixated on one aspect and eliminate other plausible explanations. That makes it doubly harder, later, to change course.

Roman had messaged me earlier that he expected a partial tracing of phone records to be done by the next morning. That will give us additional information to add to our case log.

I make myself a sandwich in the kitchen. In the middle of it, Keisha, my roommate walks in. I am sharing an apartment because I like having some company after work. Moreover, Rohan and I have been dating for not very long and I don't have any plans to live together. Too early to commit.

Mei is a fashion designer, with a great combination of artistic skills and a knowledge of the latest technology that can bring those designs to life.

'Hard day at the office?' she asks. Mei knows that I can't really discuss my work in too much detail.

'One of those days; reminds me why I took up the job,' I reply.

'It was on the news that a young woman had been found murdered.'

'Yes, another unfortunate waste of a life. The whole department is engaged. Hopefully, we'll have some answers soon,' I give out as much information as I can, knowing it all sounds a bit cagey.

'Well, hope you get some rest,' she wishes me, as she retires to her room.

I finish eating the sandwich and head back to my room. If today was busy, the next few days promise to be pretty hectic, what with Roman having to divide his time between the investigation and his testimony in court.

The cell rings in my shorts pocket and I fetch it out. It's my mother.

'Anju, are you coming on Sunday?' she inquires.

'That's the plan, unless work intervenes,' I assure her.

'Ash is really looking forward to seeing you. It's been three weeks since you came by. He really misses you,' Ash is my younger brother, Ashwin. He is much younger than I am, now a junior in high school.

'I know, mom. I've missed Ash and you and dad. I'm really going to try this weekend. Even if it's only for a few hours.'

My mother hangs up after making sure that I am avoiding too much junk food. I spend some more time on the photographs and my case notes until I figure I have pretty much gotten a good grasp of the situation. Not that it's complete. There's so much missing but I will wait for more facts to come to light rather than fill in all the blanks prematurely.

Chapter IV

Samuel

It's a chilly morning. I arrive early at the location but find there is already a line formed. It will be more than an hour before they open. I wonder when the first person came to the head of the line. It must be well before I arrived. The people in the line are anxious but friendly. Many are chit-chatting.

I am feeling a bit weak. I've not been myself last few weeks. Trying to make do, living on the street is not easy. Hence, the hot meals that the church gives out is what I look forward to, just like the folks standing here with me.

The volunteers are going about their tasks, so much energy. And they are the most friendly folks you will meet. To make it easier and more comfortable during the wait, there is a tea and coffee stand. I help myself to a cup of coffee. The warmth is welcome.

I've been coming here for the last few months and I've noticed the line has been getting longer. I don't know if it's the after-effects of the pandemic or the economy or a combination. I know my own personal problems have put me in this situation. Believe me, I know. And I will work on them. Somehow find a way. But in the meantime, I need the help I am getting from these wonderful people.

I am a little self-conscious about my clothes. My coat is from my college days when I was two sizes smaller and my shoes are not exactly in the best shape. The coffee has been helpful but I am really glad they are not starting to serve the meals. I am a bit far in the queue. Still, we are moving steadily along and soon its my turn. The gracious young lady is filling up the plate. She has a kind smile and looks at me to ask what I want. I am feeling weaker than I did before. I point out rather than say. I notice the name on her volunteer badge. 'Tina'. Beautiful name. She fills up my plate and hands it to me.

It is at this instance that I have a memory gap in my mind still. The next thing I remember is waking up in a room that looks to be inside the church. I am lying on a bed with a blanket and a pillow under my head. Its comfortable. Someone is sitting in a chair and notices that I am now awake.

I look closely and notice it's the same young woman who was serving me. Tina.

'How are you feeling?' the young lady asks me.

'I'm ok. How long have I been here?'

'About five or six minutes. There's an ambulance on the way. I think you should get yourself checked out.'

I shake my head.

'Please call it off. I don't need an ambulance. And sorry about the mess I made earlier. I don't remember much, though.'

'Don't worry about it. I have got your meal for you. Whenever you're ready,' she says reassuringly. I see she has got the meal that I was going to have.

I persuade her to cancel the call for the ambulance. I don't need to be stuck with a bill. I know what I need to do to get back to picking up my life.

'Thank you for your kindness. My name is Samuel, by the way,' I say to her.

'You are very welcome, Samuel. Tina, as you may have noticed. I hope you feel better. Please don't hesitate to call me if you need help with anything,' she hands me her card, with an address of a law firm.

I thank her, finish my meal and leave.

This has been a wake-up call.

Chapter V

Anjie

Gilchrist College

Gilchrist College is located near the downtown core of Kansas City. The campus is easy to distinguish from the surroundings just by the architecture. The closest resemblance I can see is to the Oxford University campus in England. There is a feeling that you are going back in time. Until you see the state-of-the-art parking meters and interactive booths for visitors to help them reach their destination.

I have driven to the campus with John. We have set an appointment with the president - Charles Goodwin.

We walk to the main office and enter by the huge wooden doors.

I walk up to the receptionist, show her our badges and identify ourselves.

'We have been expecting you,' she informs us as she picks up the phone, presumably to inform the president of our presence.

'You can go in, it's the second on the right,' she informs us, pointing to the corridor.

Mr. Goodwin is in his office and gets up to greet us.

'This has cast a pall on our campus. A real tragedy. What can I do to help?' he asks us, his voice sounding forlorn.

'We're very sorry for your loss, Mr. Goodwin. What we would like is to get some information on Ms. Adams, concerning her academic activities and any other activities she may have been involved in,' John replies.

Goodwin works on his keyboard and reads some information.

'I have gone into Ms. Adams' academic record here. I don't know if I'm allowed to discuss her grades particularly, but I can tell you she had an excellent academic record. I don't see any blemish. What I can do is give you a list of the courses she had taken. I don't see any problem with that.'

'Was she involved in any activities outside her studies? Any community involvement?' I inquire.

'We don't keep a list of students' involvements in non-academic activities, unless those are part of the curriculum. From what I know, Tina was involved in the theater group run by the law school students. I can get you the name of the group director. Other than that, I believe she was involved in some volunteer activities but I don't have specific information.'

'It would be helpful if you can supply us the names of professors, advisers and any other personnel she interacted with,' John adds.

'Yes, certainly,' Goodwin assures us.

'Was she working anywhere? Is there a requirement of an internship for law school?' I try to follow up on the material we found in her apartment.

Goodwin scans the information on his workstation and looks at us.

'An internship is a requirement for getting a law degree. Tina was working at the offices of Lambert & Burnham as a law intern. Regarding the details of her work, perhaps her employer and faculty adviser may be able to help further.'

Goodwin has given us names of two of her professors. Prof. Kulkarni, who was one of her current professors and Prof. Nunes, who was her former professor and counselor.

We step out of the building into the gloomy atmosphere, the gloominess enhanced by the cloudy, drizzly day.

I check my phone for new messages. There are a few from Lambert & Burnham.

'Tina's law firm has messaged back. The partners can meet us today at our convenience,' I inform John.

Both the professors are very helpful. Tina Adams has certainly a reputation universally as a good student and turns out that she had a creative mind when it came to staging theater. But neither professor can vouch for Tina's whereabouts outside of the college.

On the way to the law firm office, I see that there is a message from the ME. They will be able to give us information regarding the tod.

Lambert & Burnham

We approach the office building of Lambert & Burnham. Taking the elevator, we go into the office and are ushered into a room with a soft carpet and chairs. It seems to be soundproofed; our voices are reduced to hushed whispers. Makes sense for a place where conversations are supposed to remain confidential.

After a short wait, the door opens and two men walk in. I put the age of both somewhere in the mid to late forties. Both are wearing grey suits, making it look like they are brothers.

'I am Neil Burnham and this is Donald Lambert. We're the senior partners.'

We introduce ourselves.

'We're very sorry for your loss,' I offer condolences on behalf of us both.

'What kind of work was Ms. Adams involved in?' John starts by asking.

'Tina was part of our mergers and acquisitions team. They are responsible for analyzing the proposed merger or acquisition, from all sides, and advising our clients accordingly. I can say, without exaggeration, that we have one of best teams in this part of the country.'

'Was Tina working on anything specific?'

'There is an acquisition we are working on at the moment. The details will be finalized very soon, I think. It involves a financial services firm and our client is interested in acquiring the firm to leverage their lines of business. Tina was integral to the bid that is to be submitted.'

'Was there anything that stood out to you?'

Lambert steps in.

'This is a bid that has two prospective buyers. Our client has the edge in terms of experience in the geography and subject matter expertise. But still, stock price is going to be a key factor. That being said, every aspect needs to be solid, with ESG and crucially, integrating the acquired company so you don't end up with mass layoffs.

'We were studying a similar merger that happened a few months ago, with two suitors for a financial services firm that had a footprint close, if not exact, to what we have now. Unfortunately, that acquisition did not end successfully for our client; surprisingly so, in my opinion. We were studying that transaction to see what kind of bid to put together in this case.'

'Why was that transaction surprising?' I am curious.

'Well, it's hard to have concrete evidence, we're dealing with counterfactuals. In that case, the share price offered was identical but we were convinced that our client would be able to expand that operation, just on the basis of their areas of expertise. However, it ended up going the other way. In less than a year, nearly twenty percent of the workforce was let go. I think our client would have done much better.'

'If you don't mind my asking, how much are we talking about here? I mean in the size of the acquisition and what you stand to gain?'

'To give you a ballpark, the total cost of the acquisition stands at around two billion dollars. Our fee, all included, would be around forty million dollars.'

There is a moment of silence as we digest that piece of information.

'That's a large sum of money involved. Is it possible that someone might try to sabotage the deal or try some maneuvers to hijack it?'

'Anything is possible. Now, we assume that the personnel involved are acting in the best interests of the company. If that's not the case, all bets are off. Even so, it would be difficult for a single person to influence the outcome. I mean, if we are talking bribery, the bribe would need to be pretty hefty to overcome the potential profit from the deal, especially over the long term.'

'Was Tina seeing anyone over here, romantically I mean?' I pursue.

'No, I am quite sure she was not. We made some inquiries as well, in that regard.'

As we leave the office, I look back.

'If we want to follow the money, there's a lot of it to follow here,' I remark to John.

He nods.

'Enough to make people do things they normally wouldn't do.'

I get back to my office to find Hansie sitting in a chair. He seems to be in a good mood, always a good sign. That means he has some positive news. We could use some, right about now.

'Anjie, how's your day going so far?' he asks me, more rhetorically than really expecting an answer.

'You got something that may make it better?' I ask back.

He smiles.

'That depends. I have some information on the phone trace from Tina's cell and some more on the tire tracks we found. Rather, the flattening of the grass.

'So, let me start with the phone trace. We have traced back to thirty days. That was put on a priority. The earlier traces will take more time. Anyway, I have a complete list of the incoming and outgoing calls here in this folder,' he informs me, tapping the folder that is in front of him.

He continues:

'Here, get this, on the day of her murder, Tina received a phone in the evening, around seven-thirty. Now, we tried to trace the number but ran into a dead end. That means its most likely a burner. I haven't been able to get a name against this number. There are some other calls during the day, before and after this call. But those I was able to place with individual names.'

'That's interesting. Have you checked whether this number appears anytime before the last thirty days?' I ask.

'I checked the last ninety days for this particular number. No hits,' he says confidently.

Well, I don't expect all the answers to land in my lap, like I said. I'm thankful for any piece of good news, however small.

Mom

I turn into the narrow cul-de-sac and drive along past the houses. Just before coming to the end of the alley, I turn onto the driveway of the house on the right. This is my parents' house. To me, it will always be home. Not that I live here, I have my own apartment, with a roommate, who you met some time ago. I do have a room here though and I will always have my own room.

Every time I drive here, I am thankful that the house is not visible from the street. Because, it's the biggest house on the block, with a large front yard and a huge backyard. It reminds me of the homes they show on TV shows, the ostentatious homes belonging to celebrities. And I think that is synonymous with conspicuous consumption. This house isn't really on that scale but I think, for three, or even four, people, it just has more space than you could ever need. However, the space inside has been utilized fully. My father has his home office in the basement, from where he worked all through the pandemic; his downtown office could not be opened during the lockdowns. My mother has her own office as well, for phone and video appointments with patients.

My father has his own software development firm. He worked in Silicon Valley for almost a decade. The family moved to Kansas City when my mother got a job in one of the hospitals here. She is a doctor, ob/gyn. I know, this sounds like a stereotypical Indian American family. Perhaps I have taken a different path as an act of rebellion. I think there is some work for a shrink here. I'm not sure where my brother will want to go.

I turn into the driveway and park my Subaru Outback behind my mother's Buick. I love my car; it was six years and 80,000 miles when I bought it but drives beautifully. My dad's decade old – and looking every bit the age – F-150 is on the other side of the driveway.

The doors of the three-car-garage are all closed. One side is taken up with all the tools and materials my dad uses for this wood and metal work. He has quite a collection of saws, drills, measurement devices and the latest accessories you can find. Sometimes I think he likes to use the tools more than the products he makes. He is quite handy, though. Quite a bit of the furniture in the house has been made in the garage and the quality is unimpeachable. If anyone compliments him on his work, his usual reply is:

'I'm competing with the Amish. Still a ways to go.'

I let myself in with the key that is always on my key-chain. I enter and peep into the living room. My father is seated there with two young men, all of them with their laptops open in front of them.

I recognize of the men. His name is Vinay. More on that in a moment. The other I am seeing for the first time. I can feel their eyes on me. I'm wearing leggings and a loose-fitting shirt, with comfortable sneakers, my hair loose at the back. My hair goes around six inches below my shoulders and even though it takes some effort to wash and style, I can't bear the thought of cutting it short, nothing like a pixie cut.

'Anju!' my father exclaims as he sees me.

'Dad!' I walk over to him and give him a hug and a kiss.

'Hello, Anjali, how are you doing?' Vinay greets me.

'Hi, Vinay, I'm good. How's it going with you?'

'Great,' he replies with a smile.

'Tim, my daughter Anjali. Anjali, Tim. Tim is working on the new app we are developing,' my father does the introduction.

We give each other a firm handshake.

'I'll see you in a bit,' my father says. I glide inside, feeling the young men's eyes following me.

I am glad my father didn't mention my job. I find that most of the men I meet are intimidated by the mention of my being a police officer.

'You're going to drive away all prospects of a love life even before I get to know anyone,' I had complained.

My mother had agreed.

'Maybe we should keep that for Anju to mention, when she wants to,' she had suggested and my father had agreed, thankfully.

Vinay and I dated for a while, a year and a half I think it was. He is a Duke guy and worked with one of the big firms before joining my father's firm. We met at a company event. I was a just a year on the force. We got to chatting and I was surprised to hear that he was a semi-pro MMA fighter. He even has done some bare-knuckles fighting, where it is legally allowed.

But you would never guess if you met him. He is the gentlest person you are likely to meet. And that holds true in bed as well. He is a Blue Devils fan, through and through. All our dates during Duke basketball games were either in front of the telly or in a sports bar.

So, what went wrong? I'm not sure myself. It's an old cliché, but with law enforcement, the job comes first. I think the accumulation of all the canceled dates took its toll. Although Vinay never complained, I could feel his disappointment and I think the guilt I felt weighed increasingly on my mind. Finally, we decided to break up. It was very amicable. I think we are friends. I also think Vinay may be ready to get back together, maybe in the hope that things will be better this time. But I'm not sure about that. There's a reason we broke up and I have a feeling, things will end the same way again, or worse; a case of history repeating itself.

Rohan and I have been seeing each other for some time now. I don't like keeping exact tallies of dates, too much effort for no reason. Where is that going and how is it going to end up? We shall see. But the circumstances under which we met make it different to any other relationship I ever had. I may narrate that tale sometime.

I walk down the corridor to the family room. Mom is sitting on a couch watching a Hindi-language series. She is multitasking as well, carrying on a phone conversation with one of her friends and I can discern it's about the outrageous developments in the drama series.

She sees me come in and quickly signs off. I give her a hug.

'I was expecting you a little earlier,' she says in a light-hearted rebuke.

'Slept in a bit longer than I planned to. What's happening in *Imlie*?' I am genuinely interested.

'It will take too long to explain. I just follow the developments as they come along.'

'Dad is working,' I point out.

Yeah. Vinay and Tim are lead developers for the new app. AI-based market analytics. That's all I know. They want to be first-to-market.'

'Looks like Olive Garden will have to wait, then. What's for lunch?'

'Something special since you're here. I've got *chicken biryani, srikhand* and *puri*,' mother replies.

I groan. That's the problem with lunch with mom. Too good to skip and then there's the guilty feeling afterward of having indulged oneself.

'If I eat all that, how am I going to chase the bad guys?'

'Hit the gym afterwards. If you are going to stay for the day, we may go out in the evening.'

'We'll see. Is Ashwin upstairs?'

'Yes. He's in his room.'

I head upstairs and knock on the door. Ashwin lets me in and I see that he is only the computer chatting with someone. I hope those are his friends and not an anonymous chat room. At his age, the possibility of meeting bad dudes online is quite high.

Ashwin signs off and I give him a hug.

'Are we going out for lunch?' he asks.

'Dad's working, we're having srikhand puri.'

He seems ambivalent.

'I really wanted to go out.'

'I'll talk to mom then if we can go out for a late lunch. Save the srikhand for dinner.'

'Ok,' he seems to be lost in some thoughts.

After a few moments of silence, I ask him.

'Is there something on your mind? You can tell me. I'm your sister first, police officer after.'

He shakes his head. I wonder what it could be. But given the fact that he is still in his mid-teens, it could be a million things and I couldn't make a guess, however hard I might try.

Chapter VI

Samuel

I look up at the order sheet that has been clipped overhead on the stove assembly. Eggs benedict. I must confess this is a personal favorite and I make it for myself quite regularly. It's a real meal, breakfast or brunch. I use Canadian bacon, never ham. Soon, the brunch and lunch hours are over and the place quiets down. It's a small café, our busiest times are breakfast and lunch. When Tasha, the only server for the slow hours, asks to take some time off for a personal matter, I say no problem. I am the chef here and now the server as well.

Its late in the afternoon when the young lady walks in. I am chatting with a customer sitting at the counter. She takes a seat by the window adjoining the street. She has a shoulder bag from which she removes a sheaf of papers. I approach the table to take her order.

She orders a coffee and a blueberry scone. This is an easy order to fill. Within a minute I am back at her table. Then she looks at me.

I'm sorry if this sounds like a bad line in a dive bar, but do I know you from somewhere?' she asks.

I am not sure, although I do get a sense of having seen her before.

'I don't think so, ma'am,' I answer best I can.

She seems to accept it but shakes her head slightly. A few minutes later, I am passing by her table when she speaks to me.

'Excuse me, I don't want to be intrusive. But I think I remember you from the church around a year ago. You were not feeling well that day. I always wondered how things turned out, especially since you refused medical attention.'

That brings a flood of memories. The shop is now empty save for one customer who is sipping her tea on the counter. I ask if it is ok to join her at the table.

'I'm sorry I didn't recognize you. I think you're the one who was handing me my plate when I fell. I do appreciate it. I meant to come by and thank you one of these days but never had a chance,' I begin with my apology.

'That's ok,' she says, 'Samuel, isn't it? I remember your name. I'm Tina.'

We shake hands.

'I'm glad to see you're doing well. You work here now?' Tina inquires.

'I'm the chef here. On slow days, slow times, I wait on customers as well.'

Tina nods appreciatively.

'Well, really nice to meet you again. It's made my day a lot more pleasant.'

I take my leave and she gets back to her papers.

In some time, she comes to the counter to pay.

'It's on the house, ma'am. I appreciate your service,' I tell her.

'Why, thank you. And it's just Tina. I really think you ought to let me pay.'

'Not this time, Tina. I hope you visit again and then you can pay like everyone else.'

Chapter VII

Anjie

The Theater Group

It is getting dark in the evening as I walk toward the theater hall of Gilchrist College. The campus is not completely deserted, some couples are canoodling on the benches, some are going through notebooks, sitting on the grass or chugging on a Starbucks. I am dressed casually in jeans and a short-sleeve t-shirt, with a Helly Hansen training top. I find that fitting in with the ambience helps gain better information and more cooperation than the official outfits. The concrete walkway leads to a double-door entrance. I push the door open and climb the ornate staircase to the second floor. The entrance to the main stage is open and I step inside.

A rehearsal is in progress. The director is sitting in the front row, barking out instructions to the actors. She stands up as I approach.

'Hi, I'm Debra. We spoke on the phone.'

'Yes, we did. I'm Detective Vilekar,' I display my badge.

'The rehearsal is just about getting over. We had to do a few more takes than I thought at first. Are you ok to wait?'

I watch as the rehearsal unfolds. The scene is a law firm that is defending a tax fraud suspect in court. It looks like an office setting but the language is decidedly behind the scenes.

'That guy is so slithery, makes my skin crawl,' says one of the defending lawyers.

'The prosecution must be praying we put him on the stand,' says another of the team.

While there is a fair amount of legalese, the whole scene is meant for an audience that is not necessarily familiar with legal jargon.

After a short while, the rehearsal wraps up.

'We can go to the director's office,' Debra suggests.

'Our theater is meant as an educational and entertainment tool. As you saw, we try to go behind the scenes to explore court cases, legal opinions and anything related to jurisprudence. That's why we have named our theater group 'Irreverent, Your Honor'. While, as *legal professionals*, we honor the law, we also know that the justice system is run by humans, with all the glory and frailties that brings. Here we use theater to keep it real, sometimes jarringly so,' she explains.

'Did you work with Tina personally?'

'Yes. Tina was quite active in the theater. I remember the last play she was working on with me. It was regarding a merger. She was interested in portraying how that could be manipulated. What would be the incentive. She was still working on it. We were planning to put that into production in the next two months.'

'Do you have the script for that or any others that you worked with Tina on?'

'I have a script that I scribbled notes on. I can send that by email. I think Tina did one more play with me around six months ago. A short play. I will need to dig up that script.'

'Is there a place where she could have kept personal belongings here?'

'Not in this building. There is a building on the other side of campus where the theater participants keep personal items in small containers, mostly costumes, wigs and the like. That's located in the basement.'

'Did she interact with anyone else here in particular?'

'Well, she wanted to cast Sarah Donalds in the lead for her play. I remember her saying that Sarah was probably the best suited. I didn't really chase her reasons. We find it hard to get people to devote time for all the rehearsals.'

The building in question is supposed to be open, Debra tells me. I decide to go and take a look for myself even though it is now dark and I'm not sure how well the basement is lighted.

The building itself turns out to be without any lights. It looks like the power has been switched off for the evening. I fetch the flashlight from my purse and find my way to the stairs. The basement is pitch black. This is the kind of place that is perfect for a jump-scare. And although I don't consider myself any more paranoid than the next person, I retrieve my Glock from my purse, keeping it by my side. At the end of a long corridor, there is a large room lined with shelves that look like warehouse shelves on which are cans of paint and construction materials. Moving along, I come to the far corner, in which I see several plastic boxes stacked two or three high. Holding my flashlight in my mouth, I see names taped on top. I unstack each box one by one until I see the name 'Tina A'. I open the box and, indeed, there are several stage props inside. In addition, there is a box of crayons, a ruler, a sketch pad and an envelope containing letter size papers. I quickly glance at them, noticing that some are printouts while others have handwritten notes. I set it aside. In a corner of the container, I notice a single key, of the type that resembles a key to a locker, of the kind you might find in a gym. There is a brand that I do not recognize. I put the key in an evidence bag and into my purse. I am not sure this is any kind of evidence at all, but it needs to be checked out.

As I come out of the building, the moonlight outside feels like brilliant sunshine. I call Debra on her cell and send her a picture of the key. She has left for the day but replies that she has no idea about what the key opens.

In my apartment, I open the envelope and empty its contents onto the table. These are play scripts, one seems to be for the recent play Tina was working on. There are also some handwritten notes. One catches my eye. It mentions the name of a hotel in Kansas City with the title 'Corporate Law and Tax Updates' – as banal a name as you could find.

Is this something Tina attended, pertaining, as it did, to her official duties? A question I want answered.

Chapter VIII

Anjie

The ME

The first message I see on my desk is from the ME. The second is from Hansie, saying he has some more information from Tina's laptop. I message Hansie that I will stop by his desk in a short while. My first stop is the ME.

Btw, if you are wondering why I am not always with John, it's because working separately is sometimes best. We get more covered that way. And everything goes into the case file, every little thing, into the Field Report or Investigation Report, as it is commonly called. That's maintained online in the police cloud, encrypted and with enough security features to withstand even the most accomplished hackers, and tested by some of the best of the hacking kind in the KCPD and the FBI.

John and I also have a zoom call at the end of each day and we record that call. This is to ensure nothing falls through the cracks.

The MEs office is by the morgue. Dr. Leroy Williamson is sitting with his assistant and looks up at me when I walk in.

'Det. Vilekar, I have some news for you.'

I take my seat.

'After careful examination, I can place the tod between nine pm and eleven pm. That's the outer limits. The last meal was taken around eight pm. That's from the state of the stomach contents. The cause of death is the GSW and death was almost instantaneous. Now, I cannot say when the body was dumped in the field, but I can say that the location where the victim was found is not the place where the crime was committed. That we can say from the content of the lungs. Tina had already stopped breathing when she was placed in the grass.'

I chew on this for a moment. It only confirms what we know of as the scene of the crime. And the timing of the phone call to 911 narrows down the timeline between when the murder took place and the body was placed in the park.

'Thank you, doctors, you are the absolute best.'

My next stop is the forensics lab where Hansie will be. He is sitting at his desk, in a cubicle in which I count three laptops, three workstations and four monitors, at a first glance.

'Hey, I have some news here. I was taking a look at some of the searches Tina was doing online. Her setting is set to automatically erase all traces of any search or site that comes up. Not very helpful. Luckily, she wasn't using a cleaning program to wipe the disk clean. So, using a back door, I was able to see some of the files that she dumped or deleted. Nothing very unusual, but I did find several recent searches related to drug law, federal status – RICO and the like. There were also plenty of searches related to corporate takeovers, leveraged buyouts, stock pricing. I have a list here that states the searches in order of quantity.'

He hands me a couple of pages with the information printed. I go through it quickly.

'What about any social media?' that's always a rich vein of information.

'Ha, yes. There's not much on the laptop. Most of that activity is done from the phone. I looked at her phone contents and it looks like Tina had a couple of social media accounts. The contents were deleted regularly. I don't see much. I can send you a list of the contacts, most of them are only identifiable by their handles. We will need to do IP searches to get their identities. That will require a warrant. I can also try to get the contents of the conversations from the cloud, but that will require a warrant as well.'

I think for a moment. Hansie is a hacker and a very good one. However, he is always on the side of caution when it comes to this kind of activity. We don't want to see a case thrown out for lack of a warrant.

'Ok, I'll see what I can do,' I say to him.

'How's your team doing?' he asks. He means the competitive league I play in, two games a week.

'We're in the playoffs. Home game this week,' I answer.

'Great. Get me those warrants and I can do a real deep-dive.'

Jacob Adams residence

John and I are back for our visit with Jacob. His wife, Jennifer, is going to be there as well. That's what we have been told.

I am at the wheel as we make our way through the traffic.

'Is it me or is the ride really smoother?' I ask John.

'The more people work from home, the smoother our ride. I hope it continues. Makes the air a lot cleaner as well.'

'The family fortune makes for an intriguing angle,' I turn to the subject at hand.

The money aspect has been going around in my mind.

'Gotta consider it. We don't know the full extent of the business but money is always a factor, isn't it?'

'We're supposed to be treading on egg-shells here.'

'At least for now.'

We park in the driveway. There are two nice-looking vehicles already there, a Jaguar and an Escalade.

We don't want to take up more of their time than absolutely necessary. John starts with the questions straight away.

I am a bit surprised to learn that Tina had a large stake in the family business.

'Tina wanted to stay out of the operations. She had a smaller stake than I do, but it's still substantial,' Jacob informed.

'You are a lawyer as well, I believe?' I asked Jennifer.

'Yes, I went to Gilchrist College, School of Law as well. But that was a few years before Tina. Our paths never crossed, in school that is,' Jennifer informed us.

'You are working at a law firm as well, downtown?'

'Yes, I work at Goodman Drexler.'

Goodman, Drexler & Associates was another well-known firm in the city.

I then bring up the subject of the time of death.

'Just to try and avoid disturbing you again, can you let me know where you were on the night in question?'

'I was in my office, which is around 3 miles from here. There was a backlog of paperwork, what with the banks and all that. I think I came back home around four am,' Jacob responds.

'Do you work late often then?'

'Yes, frequently. Sometimes not as late as this but it's not unusual. We have a lot of paperwork going on, the business took a real hit during the pandemic.'

'I was on a zoom call with our partners in Japan. That started at approximately 10 o'clock. That's about lunch time in Japan,' Jennifer informs us.

'How long did it last?'

'Around half an hour. It was a short one but important nonetheless.'

'Is it normal to have meetings at that hour?' John asks.

'For our firm, it is. With the time difference, late nights and early mornings are really quite common.'

'By the way, I was wondering if you have any idea which lock this key belongs to,' I produce the evidence bag with the key I found at the storage site on campus.

Both Jacob and Jennifer look at it intently.

'I don't think we have anything that would correspond to it,' Jacob says.

Jennifer nods her head in the negative as well.

'No idea,' she says.

'Are there any personal items belonging to Tina? Did she visit often?' I ask.

'There is some of Tina's stuff in one of the barns. Nothing in the house. I can take you around if you wish,' Jacob replies.

The barn that Jacob refers to is the one to the left of the house. We step inside. It's more a large storage shed than a barn. The majority of space is taken up by farm equipment. One section contains personal effects of Tina, Jacob and other family members. I can see some army clothing in the mix.

John and I go through the material, looking for anything that may be relevant. We come up with nothing and decide to move to the other structure.

This is another large storage unit. And has far less stuff in it than the other one. Our eyes are drawn to a collection of cars. The centerpiece is a Bugatti Veyron. The Veyron is literally in the center of the collection, flanked by a Landcruiser, a Mercedes G-class, a Land Rover Defender and an Aston Martin SUV.

'Is this your collection or Jennifer's?' I ask Jacob.

'The Aston Martin and the Defender are mine. The rest are

Jennifer's. I guess you can say we both have a love for good vehicles.'

John and I nod in agreement.

I look at John. He gives me an imperceptible shrug to indicate he doesn't have anything. We thank them and make our way out.

On the way back to the precinct, I look at John.

'If Jennifer's meeting started at ten, it would be impossible for her to be the perp. Her home office is at least an hour's drive from Colver Park. To commit the crime and then dump the body, the timeline is impossible,' I muse aloud.

'I have to agree. We'll check her recording to make sure. And try to get some corroboration.'

I nod in agreement.

'We've got Jay Martineau coming in this afternoon,' I inform John.

'That's the 911 caller?'

'Yep. I'm really curious to meet him. If nothing else, then for the choice of location for a hot date.'

John smiles.

'Kinda intrigued me as well. Adventurous types.'

'That's a safe bet. His date's gonna be there as well. Lise-Anne Johnson.'

'Could be interesting.'

Lise-Anne Johnson

Lise-Anne is dressed in a track suit and sneakers. Alongside her is Jay. They don't look intimidated by the atmosphere of a police precinct.

'Let's get ourselves seated, shall we?' I suggest, leading the way to a conference room. John has joined us well.

'I'm really curious why you chose that spot at that time of night,' I address them.

The young woman, exuding the confidence of an athlete used to being the center of attention, sweeps back her hair.

'I've been there before, during the day and I always liked the quietness. It closes at seven thirty but that's more an honor system.'

'And you are Lise-Anne's boyfriend, I take it?' I address Jay.

'Not exactly,' the young man shakes his head.

'It was our first time together. I actually have a boyfriend, he's on the swim team. I play on the basketball team. Jay is a cheerleader. I hope you won't be making names public.'

'Not unless you are called in court when it goes to trial.'

'Well, *on verra*,' Lise-Anne mutters.

'Did you first spot Ms. Adams?' I ask.

'No, it was Jay.'

'So, how did that come about?' I turn to Jay.

'Well, L, that is to say, Lise-Anne, had flung my socks in the grass when we were, you know, getting ready…,' Jay seems at a loss for words.

'Please, take your time,' I say gently.

'Well, when we had finished, I went searching for my socks, using my flashlight. I saw something shining and at first, I thought it was an animal. So, I got the gun from my waistband and took off the safety. When I reached further, I saw it was a purse with decorative stones. I thought it kinda strange to see that and I let L know. We thought it might be lost by a hiker so I proceeded to see if any other items were lying around.

That's when I saw her arm. It was spooky for sure. We got to the car and called 911.'

'I actually didn't see anything. Jay said to get the f outta there and we did. We were not sure if the person who dumped the body was in the vicinity or not,' Lise-Anne adds.

'On your way in or out, did you happen to see any cars or people around the place?' John inquires.

'We did pass some cars on the main road but no one on the dirt road. And there was no car around when we got there, either. If there was someone in the grass, they were there without a car.'

A few more questions make it clear that Lise-Anne and Jay have no more information to offer. Their main concern is their surreptitious rendezvous more than anything else.

'Nice couple,' Roman remarks, as they leave.

'Quite an adventure. I have a feeling they won't be picking deserted spots for their trysts for a while.'

'Unlikely anyone would be hiding in the grass, without a car,' Roman muses.

'The body was dumped sometime before. Lucky break for the kids. If they had arrived at the same time, who knows what would have happened,' I think aloud.

Samuel (narrator)

I see her again, outside, on the sidewalk. Today, I am busy in the kitchen. Its busier. I've just stepped outside to the counter to put a fresh batch of biscotti in the shelf. Our customers like biscotti. And my brownies. I think that's my specialty. I have this unique recipe with a hint of nutmeg that just captures the essence of the chocolate. That's why I chose that as a gift for Tina when she was here last time. I am confident she must have liked them.

I see her hesitating. Is that a good sign? I'm hoping she comes in. Not sure where that will take me – and her. But I liked talking to her. That was two weeks ago. Her step, that had slowed, quickens again and she opens the door firmly. She has stepped in now. But I got to head back to the kitchen. She notices me behind the counter and gives me a quick smile and a wave. I smile and wave back. Lena will help her. She is the server.

The orders are coming in fast. A lot of them are for eggs and bacon. And toast. Breakfast items. Which our customers like to have any time of day. I get the dishes out the door fast as I can.

I step outside. Tina has taken a table by the window. I think it's the same as the one last time.

I approach her, with some trepidation, I must admit. Isn't uncertainty frightening? She is having coffee and going over documents. She looks up, sees me and smiles.

'Looks like a busier time for you today than it was the last time I was here,' she says.

'You can say that. I've got a few orders going. But I thought I'll step out and say hello before you leave.'

'Much appreciate it. And I am paying,' she smiles.

'Yes, ma'am,' I smile back. Her smile is just magnetic.

I have a feeling that Tina wants to continue the conversation. But I got to get back to the kitchen. It may be slow but there are still orders to fill.

I find her in her sitting when I come out again, after finishing up the batch.

'You think maybe we can grab a coffee somewhere other than here?' she asks.

'I was building up the nerve to ask you myself,' I respond.

My shift ends shortly after and we decide to relocate to a diner a couple of blocks away.

'I really am so happy to see you're doing well. Especially after I saw you at the church. I was worried about your health. I hope you got yourself looked at,' Tina begins.

I give a long sigh.

'I was in a rough spot then. Look, I don't want to burden you with my issues. I really do appreciate your concern. But it's been a long and rocky road.'

'Are you or were you in some kind of trouble?'

'I was an addict. I was into computers but at some point, I don't know exactly when, I feel into the addiction trap. I didn't realize it until it kind of took over. I had a steady job but I soon became too unpredictable to my employers. And then I blew away most of my savings on my habit. I was in real bad shape. By the time I realized I had to change something, I was desperate. Luckily, a former colleague of mine was able to get me into rehab. That's about the time I showed up at the soup kitchen. Been sober for more than a year now and I attend the meetings every week so I don't fall off the wagon.'

'Did you learn to cook and bake at home?'

'I always had a liking for cooking. When I was a kid, I used to try recipes from books my mom had in the kitchen. I started on the job as a waiter and filled in a couple of times when the chef called in sick. They liked my food. So, when the chef left, I got the job.'

'Is your family here in Kansas City or Missouri?' Tina is curious to know.

'My mom passed away when I was in elementary school. My dad had walked out soon after I was born. I've got some relatives in Indiana. But I'm not really in touch with them.'

Our coffee is about finished. I look at my watch.

'Tina, thank you for your concern and your kindness. I have to leave now. I'm doing some online classes in the evenings.'

'Will I see you again? I mean, not at your restaurant.'

'If you would like an exclusive dinner prepared by an up-and-coming chef, how about we make it at my place? It's not the poshest of apartments, but the food will make up for the simple décor. I'm confident of that.'

'I really would like that,' she answers.

Chapter IX

Anjie

The precinct

I knock on John's cubicle. He has an office that is twice the size of mine, with two nice chairs for visitors. He is alternately looking at his screen and some reports on his desk. He nods me to a seat.

'We don't have any hits on the bullet, yet,' he informs me.

'Have they checked all the databases?'

'IBIS is done. They don't have anything. Unless it's in the backlog waiting to be entered in the system. Nothing in Missouri either. I think they've checked a few other states as well. It will take a while for the whole thing to be done.'

IBIS is the system maintained by the Bureau of Alcohol, Tobacco and Firearms. I never quite understood the correlation between the three. Alcohol and tobacco are often treated as vices. Firearms are a constitutional right.

'Well, the good thing is they will keep it in their unresolved so we don't have to do this again,' I point out the silver lining.

Most state and federal systems run periodic checks for unmatched bullets and fingerprints. They are supposed to inform right away if they get a hit.

'That is true, although far from perfect,' John nods.

I roll my eyes. Its government bureaucracy, after all. But I have to say, it works well usually.

'I'm going to be meeting some of Tina's colleagues and faculty at Gilchrist, as we discussed,' I inform John.

He nods affirmatively.

'We need to narrow down our scope before we start asking for alibis. I'm going down to the lab shortly to check if they have anything new from the truck.'

'If the body was placed in and then dumped from the SUV, hopefully there's been some transference,' I add.

'Any progress on the key you found?'

'No, nothing. I tried a few of the public lockers around the city, no success.'

'By the way, Elsworth is asking to meet with us, wants to know how things are going. There's a lot of press and she wants to keep ahead of it all.'

'Let me know the time and I'll be there,' I answer.

I am meeting with a couple of Tina's friends over at a mall close to Gilchrist College. I want to trace Tina's movements during the evening in question and to also get to know the people she interacted with.

The parking lot is halfway full. I park my car a bit further away from the entrance. I don't like the idea of being stuck if I need to leave in a hurry.

It's a nice mall. Inside, the stores are brightly lit and I walk briskly to the food court. If you just look at the food court, you would assume the consumer economy is going really strong. I look around and spot the coffee place that we discussed earlier. We are meeting right in front of it.

In that neighborhood, I spot a young man and woman in conversation. They look up when I approach.

'Robert, Selena?' I ask.

They both nod. Robert and Selena were close pals of Tina, from the inquiries I've made. I thought it best to meet with these two to start off.

'Det. Vilekar. We talked on the phone. Are you getting anything?' I ask.

'We just got this table and we were about to get some coffee,' Marcia tells me.

'No problem. I'll get that,' I offer.

Robert accompanies me to coffee shop.

'I haven't been in this place in a while. It's a nice food court,' I remark to him.

'It's close to campus and it's got a good variety,' he says. I look around and there seems to be a good mix of cuisines. Thai, Shawarma, Chinese, Indian, American and, of course, the ever-present Subway and McDonalds.

We collect our lattes and get back to the table.

'Tina was a serious student. Not that she didn't like to have fun, but she really put in the effort,' Marcia answers when I start asking about Tina.

'Even in the plays she set for the theater group, she worked really hard,' Robert adds.

'Did you work with her in the theater or in any of her classes?'

'I was working with her on the script that we were to start performing in the next couple of months. I had the role of a banker, a corrupt banker,' Robert says.

'Anything in particular?'

'It was looking at ways a good deal could be derailed. In that sense, it was a dark play, full of venal characters. There's any number of people who would act for their own self-interest, that was the presumption.'

'Dark indeed,' I remark. Talk about a glass half empty.

'I took a couple of classes with her. We would work on case studies together,' says Selena.

'So, you three hung out together?'

'Off and on. It's not like we were always together. Robert and I have been on a couple of dates as well,' Selena says.

'And how's that working out?' I'm curious to know.

'So far, so good,' Robert replies, with a smile.

'Was Tina, like, a big party girl? What were your hangout places?'

'No, Tina was not into big parties at all. She had a bad experience when she was in high school, so she told me. She is convinced someone slipped GHB into a drink at one of the parties she went to. Luckily, for her, a friend was there and noticed her before anything worse happened. She never went to those kinds of parties. We used to hang out at cafés and some nice bars with live music.'

'Really lucky for her,' I say sincerely. Date rape is a serious problem at parties and I think everyone needs to have a friend like Tina did, looking out for them.

'Was anything bothering her? College or personal?'

'She looked bothered on and off the last few months. I think some of her grades had slipped a bit and that was bothering her as well,' Robert recalled.

'There was something she mentioned to me a few weeks back. She said she had talked to a former theater student about a matter she was working on. She didn't mention much beyond that. I don't know anything about it or what happened to the student,' Selena mentions.

'Did she mention a name or any personal details?'

'No, she didn't. She clearly did not want to share more. I didn't pay much attention. I thought I'd tell you while I remember,' Selena says, trying to recall.

'I'm glad you did. You never know where the smallest thing might lead you,' I assure her.

I show them the key that I found. Neither of them knows of any locker where it might fit.

As I get ready to leave, I remember something.

'Do you recall Tina referring to the L'Ascension Hotel here in Kansas City?'

They both shake their heads in a No.

I leave them with their lattes still unfinished and as I look back, they are both in somber conversation.

Later that evening, I am on my way back to my apartment, when I get a call from John. I have already apprised him of my meeting with Selena and Robert.

'Vilekar, I just heard from the DA. Looks like I will be on the stand tomorrow.'

'I will try to be there. How is it looking so far?'

'Hard to say. Any shooting nowadays, the state is on the back foot. Even with someone like Lloyd.'

'Well, good luck. I'll be among the back rows, if I can get a seat.'

Chapter X

Anjie

Jeremy Lloyd

I reach the courthouse mid-morning. As usual, the hallways are busy with people. Some are lawyers conferring with their clients, there are families with perhaps a loved one on trial or awaiting justice for a wrong.

The room I am seeking is tucked away in a corner. As I approach, I see a few officers from my precinct and some folks who I don't recognize. It's hard to tell whether they are in support of Jeremy Lloyd or against him. For Lloyd has done some real harm to a lot of people; young and old alike. At the same time, there are those who benefited from him as well. His entire network of drug dealers, distributors, middlemen and money launderers are probably beholden to him.

There is a short recess right about now and I am looking to find a seat. I see that behind the prosecution desk, the last three rows are mainly police officers and some news reporters. There are more reporters from social media sites than the traditional news outlets. One of the police officers signals to me that there is a seat available and I edge along the bench, finally wedging myself between two patrolmen. They are doubtless here to support their colleagues in uniform. As I take my seat, I see the judge return to her chair.

The jury takes their seats and the prosecution calls John Roman to the stand.

John is sworn in and takes the witness chair. He is dressed in a somber grey suit and blue tie, reflecting the occasion.

The DA goes over the timeline with John being called to the crime scene and then arriving to find Lloyd had been shot and then taken to hospital. The subsequent search of the vehicle found a weapon on the driver's side and a large quantity of cocaine hidden under the engine hood, taped to the underside. John had been present for the search and had taken the evidence into custody.

As soon as the direct is completed, the defense lawyer, Len Kaminsky, stands up to address the judge.

'Your honor, I would like to ask for some latitude on cross, since the witness was not just there at the scene, but is also knowledgeable on the background of Mr. Lloyd, given his prior involvement,' he asks.

'I am okay with you having some latitude as long it's not a fishing expedition,' the judge rules, showing a firm hand.

'Very well, your honor,' Kaminsky replies, with an exaggerated bow.

He addresses John. For the next few minutes, the conversation is about John's background in the military police, his experience in handling crime scenes and, finally, his work with the KCPD. John is composed and patient, answering in a calm and collected manner.

'Now, coming to the day of the shooting, specifically the day Mr. Lloyd was shot, can you tell us how your involvement started?'

'I got a notification from dispatch that officers Lohuz and Watkins were following a possible felony suspect,' John replies.

'Where were you at that moment?'

'Once I got the location, I figured I was around six or seven minutes away.'

'On hearing about the pursuit, what did you do?'

'I contacted the patrol car using my police radio. I then started driving toward the location in my vehicle.'

'Your official vehicle?'

'Yes, sir.'

'While there was this pursuit, were you apprised of the location changes?'

'Yes, sir, officer Lohuz was on the radio and communicated the progress of the pursuit, including the location.'

'How and where did the pursuit end?'

'The driver of the fleeing vehicle attempted to make a high-speed turn at the corner of Fenster and Barley streets. The vehicle skidded into a ditch by the side of the road, effectively immobilizing it.'

'When did you first come to know that the person being pursued was Mr. Lloyd?'

'That would be when I first communicated directly with officer Lohuz.'

'How did officer Lohuz know?'

'He ran the plate and the vehicle showed up as registered to Mr. Lloyd.'

'And before that, officer Lohuz and officer Watkins had no idea that the person in the car was Mr. Lloyd?'

'Not to my knowledge, no.'

'Had you encountered Mr. Lloyd before, detective, prior to this incident?'

'Yes, sir.'

'Can you please describe the circumstance of that encounter?'

'On that occasion, I had placed Mr. Lloyd under arrest.'

'What was the reason for that arrest?'

'There was a homicide which we believed to be drug-related. Our investigation led us to be believe that Mr. Lloyd had ordered the hit that resulted in the homicide. We staked out a place that Mr. Lloyd was known to inhabit. Four days later Mr. Lloyd was seen in his vehicle in the vicinity of the premises. We attempted to intercept the vehicle.'

'This place that you had under surveillance: was it an apartment or a house?'

'It was an apartment.'

'Yet, you did not see Mr. Lloyd enter or leave this apartment?'

'No, we later discovered that he had access to another apartment in an adjacent apartment building, one that belonged to one of his associates.'

'You did not see him enter that building?'

'No, we did not.'

'How came you to identify Mr. Lloyd?'

'One of the officers stationed in the vicinity made a positive id as he exited with the vehicle.'

'Can you describe the sequence of events that followed the identification by the officer?'

'I was informed by radio that Mr. Lloyd was exiting in the vehicle. We turned on the lights and sirens and followed behind the defendant. The defendant, however, sped up instead of slowing down. I attempted to bring my vehicle alongside the defendant's, at which point he opened fire. The other vehicle managed to speed up and bump the defendant's vehicle from behind, due to which it crashed into a tree that was by the side of the road. We attempted to effect an arrest. However, the defendant resisted and a struggle ensued.

After a brief interval we managed to overpower the defendant and make the arrest.'

'During the struggle, as you put it, did the defendant incur any injuries?'

'I believe he did, yes sir.'

'Injuries that required hospitalization?'

'I believe the defendant spent one night in the hospital and was released the next day.'

'What became of the charges that you had brought against the defendant?'

'Those were dismissed.'

'Why was that?'

'The DA decided that there wasn't sufficient evidence to proceed.'

'I see. Was there any consideration of the fact that excessive force had been used on Mr. Lloyd by the police and this would make it difficult to bring a conviction?'

'I wasn't made aware of any such reasoning on the part of the DA.'

'Is it fair to say, detective, that the police, and you, have an animus against the defendant. Due to the fact that he fired at a cop and was yet able to get away with it?'

'I cannot agree with that statement. At least for myself, I did not and do not harbor any such sentiments.'

At this point, Kaminsky walks over to his desk and rummages through a sheaf of papers. This is all for drama. I am anticipating his next question.

After a thoughtful search, Kaminsky carried a folder to his lectern and opens it. He then looks at John.

'During your communication with officer Lohuz, did you come to know the reason for the pursuit?'

'Yes, sir. The vehicle was being pursued due to it having a broken taillight.'

I groan inside. Broken taillights as a reason for a traffic stop have generally gotten a bad rep with the public. But then, I already knew the reason and I also have a good idea where this is leading to. So does John.

'A broken taillight. Did you consider that a sufficient reason for a high-speed pursuit?'

'It is a moving violation,' John answers.

'A minor moving violation in the eyes of the law, wouldn't you agree?'

'Kidnapping victims have sometimes broken taillights from inside the trunk to gain attention. That particular action has been counseled by some law enforcement agencies as well.'

Kaminsky takes a moment to collect himself.

'Turning our attention to the scene of the shooting, you saw that Mr. Lloyd had been shot and was in the driver's seat in his vehicle. Is that correct?'

'That is correct.'

'How much time had elapsed between the shooting and your arrival?'

'I can't say for sure. Could not have been more than 2 minutes.'

'So, by the time you arrived, the gun that was allegedly found in the car had already been retrieved by the officers. Is that a correct statement?'

'I couldn't say for sure.'

'Was the hood open when you arrived?'

'No, it wasn't.'

'But there was adequate time for the officers to open the hood and close it prior to your arrival. Is that correct?'

'Again, I wouldn't be able say that with certainty.'

'We'll come back to that.'

Kaminsky walks over to his table and picks up another folder that he hands over to John.

'Detective, I want you to take a look at the photographs in this folder. Let me know there are the ones taken at the scene of the shooting.'

John goes through the photographs and then looks up at Kaminsky.

'Yes, sir. These are photographs taken at the scene.'

'I would like you to take a look at photograph marked as CS14. Have you found it, sir?'

'Yes, I have and looking at it right now.'

'What is this a photograph of, detective?'

'It's a photograph taken from the rear of Mr. Lloyd's vehicle.'

'The license plate is visible?'

'Yes, it is.'

'And that's the license plate of Mr. Lloyd's vehicle. Is there any doubt about that?'

'No doubt.'

'And the broken taillight on the right is visible as well?'

'Yes, it is.'

'Now, this is an 8x10 photograph of the type 'surroundings': that is, it's one of the photographs of the area surrounding the defendant's vehicle. Am I correct?'

'Yes, sir.'

'At the bottom right-hand corner, about an inch to the left, can you see a faint red glow? If you find it difficult with you naked eyes, I can give you a lens.'

This is the case. Right here.

John takes the lens and spends about a minute looking at the spot Kaminsky referred to. He is taking his time knowing this is a critical moment.

'I see a faint red glow, yes sir.'

'The location of that glow is the grass along the right edge of the road. Is that correct?'

'A couple of blades of grass, that is correct.'

'And given the relative position of the vehicle, that spot with the glow is not more than three feet from the defendant's vehicle. Is that an accurate estimate?'

'In my opinion, that's an accurate estimate.'

'Can you make out the source of that glow?'

'I don't see the source.'

'Could it be a small piece of broken glass or plastic that is reflecting light?'

'It could be. It could also be the reflection of a light from a police car.'

'All the same, detective, it could be from a piece of red glass or plastic?'

'I would be speculating, sir. I don't think I have sufficient information to form a judgment either way to answer your question.'

'I understand detective.'

Kaminsky has now adopted the mannerism of a school teacher trying to reason with a recalcitrant student.

'Given your testimony here today, detective, do you really expect us to believe that officers Lohuz and Watkins started the pursuit because they saw a car with a broken taillight?'

The prosecution lawyer springs from his seat.

'Objection, your honor, calls for speculation. Detective Roman cannot be expected to know what Mr. Kaminsky and whoever he includes in his 'us' believe.'

The judge sustains the objection.

Kaminsky then tries another tack.

'If I put forward a theory of what transpired that day which goes like this:

'Officers Lohuz and Watkins are waiting for Mr. Lloyd. They see him drive away and start pursuing. Unobtrusively, to begin with. Then, after encountering an isolated stretch, they move closer and put on the light and siren. Mr. Lloyd panics, especially given his history with the police. He tried to make a hasty turn and lands his car in a ditch. The officers then exit their vehicle. Officer Lohuz rushes toward Mr. Lloyd. Officer Watkins breaks the taillight and disposes of the pieces. Mr. Lloyd makes some kind of movement or no movement. Officer Lohuz shoots him through the window. In any case, Mr. Lloyd does not have the weapon in his hand. The officers plant the gun and then retrieve and seize it. They call the ambulance and that's when you arrive.

Is that a satisfactory theory, detective?'

The prosecuting attorney objects again but the judge allows the question.

'That's a completely unsatisfactory theory. It begins with the assumption of a conspiracy and then escalates to a pre-meditated shooting and manipulation of evidence. I don't believe that's what happened here at all.'

'Nevertheless, it is possible?'

'Anything is possible. But I'm not inclined to give it any credence.'

John has stood firm but Kaminsky has planted the seeds of doubt in the minds of the jurors. To what extent the seeds take root will determine the verdict.

I wait in the hallway as John finishes his testimony and steps out. He sees me and comes over.

'A bit of a shitshow. Kaminsky is making Lloyd look like a victim here. That little reddish spot could have been anything.'

I give John a squeeze on the shoulder.

'You did well,' I try to point out the positive.

I don't say what I'm sure is going through both of our minds: the jury might well find Kaminsky's argument more persuasive than the state's.

'Anyway, I'm going to grab a coffee and head on to the station,' John tells me.

'I've had enough coffee for the day. I'll see you there.'

There is an email from Elsworth asking to see me.

'The lab is done with the purse and contents. We can return to the next of kin,' she hands me Tina's purse. It's in a sealed plastic bag, 'Handle with care' is written on a label.

'That would be Jacob.'

Elsworth shrugs her shoulders.

'The family would appreciate having it back. It's the least we can do.'

John is busy when I pop into his cabin. I find him studying some documents on his workstation. He looks up at me.

'Going over my testimony. I was just trying to see if anyone significant was left out in the direct.'

'Is there anything?'

'I don't think so, no. But I am going to over this and my case notes.'

That's a signal that he won't be available for some time. I decide it's better to return the purse sooner rather than later.

I call Jacob's cell. He is at his office. His office location is not too far away from the family residence. The office itself is a two-story building. I see some lights on. There is parking in the front of the building.

There are just a couple of vehicles out here. I try the main entrance to the building. The door is locked and I don't see anyone on the front desk. Not surprising. It's quite late in the evening now. Instead of calling Jacob's cell, I walk around to the back of the building. Here, I see there is another parking lot. There are a handful of SUVs and some farm vehicles. The farm equipment vehicles have the company logo prominently painted on the driver side door.

There seems to be no entrance from the back of the building. I walk to the front and call Jacob's cell. In a couple of minutes, he comes down and lets me in. His office is on the second floor, one of the lights that I observed earlier. We take the steps. His is a corner office, at the end of a corridor. As we make our way, I make a mental note of some of the names I see on plaques outside.

'Tina's purse, Mr. Adams. We won't be needing it further for our investigation.'

'Thank you, detective. I appreciate your coming down here. Any progress, any leads? We are hoping you guys come up with something soon.'

'We're following some promising leads. We will keep you informed of any developments.'

I strive to give Jacob as much information as possible on the investigation as I can, without going into specific details. He is an immediate family member entitled to expect a thorough investigation and pursuit. At the same time, we have not yet ruled him out as a possible suspect.

Jacob places the purse in his briefcase and listens to my summary. He has a few questions of his own and I can see he is frustrated about not getting the level of detail he is seeking from me. I leave his office about half an hour later, trying to once again memorize the names that are posted along the corridor.

Chapter XI

Samuel

It is a beautiful day. A gorgeous day of sunshine has turned into a delectable evening, a light hazy glow of the setting sun accompanied by a breeze that seems to bring the fragrance of the trees and flowers into the streets. Is nature feeling different today or is it me that is looking at everything with a new mood.

Our café is closed. But I am busy in my own kitchen. The apartment is modest, the neighborhood falls in the same category. I live on a street of condominium buildings. There is a small park nearby where you will see kids playing in the evenings and new mothers pushing strollers during the day. Some construction activity is going on nearby. The traffic is going to get worse for sure.

My place is far from fancy but I have tried to splurge on the kitchen. When I say splurge, I mean in relative terms. The counter tops are butcher block. I do not want to worry about damaging the granite when I am cutting and chopping. There is a good feel to wood as well. It takes you back to the ancient kitchens of Rome or Paris, when none of the fancy stuff like quartz even existed.

The *piece de resistance* is the stove. It has six burners and a grill. The burners have enough firepower to compete with a small restaurant. This set me back a bit. To make up for it, my bedroom is really bare-bones. There is a 12-inch futon and a night stand. With a small closet.

I have thought long and hard about what to prepare for this occasion. At the end, I have decided to go with English pot roast. Made in a Dutch oven to avoid losing any of the flavor. There is something classical about that dish. As you may have guessed, I am old school. For this to work, the main ingredient has to be perfect or near-perfect. And you have to be prepared to spend some time finding the exact cut. No comprising with boneless chuck. You may need to spend a few hours extra or a few dollars more but, let me assure you, it's well worth it.

My recipe is my secret. A magician doesn't tell. After the pot roast, I think it's the rosemary that you need to decide on. How much, when? Rosemary is a strong, flavorful herb. Too much, it can easily overwhelm the dish. But you need the taste to come through as well. The chef's got to decide.

The dish is only as good as the appetizer. Things got to flow. I spent a long time mulling over the soup. In the end, it was lentil soup that won the day. Now, with a pot roast, you don't want an appetizer that is too heavy. Just something to whet the appetite. I think lentil soup is best for that, not to mention that, pound for pound, it has great protein content. And nothing like some coconut milk to make you think of the sea, even in the middle of Kansas City!

And then the dessert. You might have guessed. But that's for later. A little extra, since it's chez Samuel.

The doorbell rings. I've been waiting for this moment. Ever since we had that conversation at the little diner. And Tina is now standing here. Her blond hair is in a bob cut, harkening back to an era of style and elegance. And the dress is, as always, just right for the occasion.

There is soft music going on in the background. The sound system is the latest in surround sound. You can't help but feel the music permeating your body and soul. At the table, I have a beautiful flower vase with magnolias and orchid.

The dinner is amazing and I can see that Tina is impressed. We take our time. There is so much to talk about. And I think we both feel the heat slowly rising. And there, I think you can imagine the rest. I am not one to kiss and tell. Did I mention I am old school? Pretty sure I did.

Tina leaves about an hour later. Exhausted, I fall asleep, the dishes will have to wait.

Chapter XII

Anjie

The lawyers' conference

It's that time in the afternoon. I don't know how to describe it. The pace of everything around me seems to be frenetic. I don't know if that's because we're all trying to clean up our desks before we leave or that the mornings rarely go as planned. In any case, I find the middle of the afternoon a distinctly productive time of day. I'm chugging my third coffee of the day or maybe the fourth. I find it preferable to getting a sugar rush.

I see a text message on my cell. It's from Robert. That would be Tina's friend, who I met along with Selena, at the mall. The message doesn't say much beyond Robert wanting to talk to me.

'Robert, detective Vilekar,' I have called him back first chance. I'm not one to let grass grow under my feet if I can help it.

'Hello, detective. I remembered something that I thought could be helpful. I'm not sure that it is and didn't strike me until last evening. But I thought I should mention it, nonetheless.'

'It could well be important and helpful.'

'I remember one time; we were talking about the play that we were working on. I think we discussed some of that last time. Anyway, as you know, there's all kinds of skullduggery depicted in that play. So, we were going over the script, line by line, and I made a remark, something along the lines of – 'Aren't we exaggerating a bit here?'. And Tina looks at me and says – 'No, not at all. Just look at the lawyers' conventions, like the one that happened in our city. I think we're on the tame side, if anything'. I didn't think much of it and it never occurred to me that it was anything specific that she was referring to.'

I try to digest this information. At first glance it does not strike me as of any great significance. But this is a young woman's death I am working on. Anything and everything is to be treated as significant and pertinent until I can confidently rule it out.

'This convention, did Tina mention any particular specific name for it like, maybe, a Tort lawyers' convention?'

'I don't think she did. I would've remembered it if she had. And I didn't think to ask either.'

'How about a location, or a date. Did she say anything about when or where?'

'All I can say is that it was in the city. That's what she said.'

My mind is racing. I am thinking of the L'Ascension Hotel, the entry that Tina had made in the margins of her play script. It's nebulous, though. L'Ascension is one of the top-rated luxury hotels in the city and I reckon there is more than one convention occurring there every week. Most of these are meant to be boondoggles, meant as rewards for employees, with fine dining and golf being the staple. There is plenty of other business on the side as well, with Vice taking a look on occasion.

Given that Tina was a law student, I am also thinking of the possibility that someone she knew was attending this convention. Having a name would go a long way to narrowing down the details.

'Is there anyone she mentioned as taking part in this convention, as a participant or presenter or in any other capacity?' I ask.

'Sorry, no. I wish I could help more. But I really don't have anything to add. As I said, I was doubtful this information was helpful or even relevant.'

'It's too early to decide that. Let me work on this and I will call you if I need your assistance.'

I hang up and get back to the task I was working on when Robert called – completing my field reports on current investigations. I will run down this new development as well. I know better than to expect that it will be easy.

It's late in the evening when the field reports are finally done. It's not just writing the reports, though they are in extreme detail, the filing part is no cakewalk either. There is considerable metadata connected to each incident or interview. Elsworth is very particular, as she should be.

I turn my attention to lawyers' conventions in KC. A Google search. Not surprisingly, there are too many entries to go into any kind of detail. I try to narrow down using the name of the hotel. Here, I see a few entries but I doubt this list is exhaustive. The entries are few and far between. I am not sure what kind of filters to use either. After an hour of this back and forth, I call the hotel and identify myself. A very helpful sounding lady comes on the line and assures me that they will do all they can to help.

'Do you have an online register where you keep a list of all the meetings and conventions at your hotel?' I ask her.

'Yes, we do. But it's on our intranet.'

'Does that mean I will need to come over there to take a look?'

'Yes, that's what I would suggest. The alternative is to print all the records and send them over to you.'

'How many of these are we talking about, say for the last six months?'

The lady pauses for a few seconds.

'I would say between around a hundred-fifty. That's just a ballpark.'

I can envision a dozen boxes stuffed in my office and John's and maybe spilling over into Elsworth's.

'Ok, that's fine. I will stop by. And I will give you a heads-up before that.'

I think for a moment and then call Robert.

'How familiar are you with lawyers and law firms in the city?' I ask him.

'I am familiar with most of the big firms. And the big names. I know some of the smaller ones as well but not all of them. We have some law professors who may know a lot more.'

'I'm wondering if you can come with me to the hotel tomorrow. I want to narrow it down by participants. It may take a few hours.'

'Sure,' Robert replies.

I'm on my way home when I start thinking about dinner. There is not much in the fridge. I stop on the way at a salad and sandwich shop and pick up a garden salad. I've got some vinaigrette that I can use on this. A salad and a pot of chamomile tea. That should set me up nicely for a few hours.

I'm used to getting by on salads and tea from my days in gymnastics. The sensitive weigh-in scales could catch a fraction of an ounce. And an ounce is a big deal. I think things have changed over the last few years but every coach wants to get gold and they will do anything short of breaking the rules to do that. Some of the unscrupulous ones will go that far as well. Many a gymnast goes to bed hungry just to get the weigh-in. That daily weigh-in habit has stayed with me, but now, a tenth of an ounce doesn't produce the same anxiety as it did then.

Changing into my shorts and halter top, I open my laptop, the salad and tea within reach. Taylor Swift is playing in the background. There is an email from Hansie. I've asked him to run a background check on some of Tina's acquaintances. He lets me know he hasn't come up with anything yet but he still has a few databases to go. I make a note to follow up with him next chance I get.

I am trying to cram the list of law firms and the well-known lawyers as quickly as I can. If I can avoid cross-referencing names between lists, that would make the effort more doable. Between myself and Robert, I am hoping we can identify someone who Tina may have suspected of something unsavory. What that is, I'm not sure.

I think I've gone through around twenty of the top law firms in the city when I decide to call it a day. I resolve to get back on it after my morning exercise routine. I take a quick hot shower. Funny how a shower works. It can get your energy level up or down, almost like it knows what you need. Right now, I definitely need to get my energy level way down. I dry myself, quickly gulp down the remaining tea and hit the sack. It must not be more than a minute before sleep takes over.

Chapter XIII

Anjie

The Luc Tyler assassination

As they say, the best laid plans…..

I've been asleep for barely two hours when the cell phone ring puts paid to that continuing. I roll over to my left and pick up the phone. As expected, John is on the line.

'Vilekar, we have a shooting. I'll send you the address.'

The address is just off the 350. From my apartment its going to be a twenty-five-minute drive, hopefully less. I am out of bed before the call has ended. A quick change of clothes and I'm ready to go. The morning exercise routine and the rest of the law firms will need to wait.

Siren wailing, I speed down the 70 and take south on the 435, on to the 350. The traffic is light and I cover the distance quickly. The flashing lights are like a guide. Two patrol cars are on the scene. I park my car to the side and walk to the where the officers are. I know them well. They recognize me and nod in my direction. One is a rookie, the other is an old hand.

The victim has been declared dead at the scene. The ambulance is not an option. The body will be kept until forensics have collected the evidence. The ME's office will then take it to the morgue for an autopsy.

'Detective Roman's on his way. Anyone else coming?'

'We have vice on the way as well. We got a hit on the vic. Known drug dealer. Found a gun behind on the seat.'

'Any id on the assailant?'

'Nothing yet. No eyewitnesses. Someone heard the shots and called it in.'

They hand me the id they have checked. A drivers license. I recognize the name.

Luc Tyler.

The gun is a snub-nosed .38, a popular choice among dealers and gang members. Easy to conceal and enough firepower to be effective from a moderate distance. It is now in an evidence bag.

'Fired recently?'

'No, not in this instance.'

Luc has been on the police radar for a while now. A suspect in homicide, aggravated assault, distribution and trafficking. One could say that this is all in a day's work for those in this line of work. He who lives by the sword etc. This is just part of the story, a sometimes-misleading part. We need to find the motive and the person/organization behind. Bad as Luc may have been, he could very well be replaced by someone badder and more powerful. And that doesn't bode well. This homicide may be a precursor to an ugly war over territory. Preventing it may not be easy. Time will tell.

Luc is in the driver's seat, I can see at least three bullet wounds in the upper torso, the blood staining his light-colored blazer. The force of the gunshots has pushed his upper body almost onto the passenger seat. The seat belt is the restraint that still holds it from going completely over. Given the ambient light as well as the dark interior of the car, it's difficult to say whether the bullets have been lodged in the victim or gone through. In either case, the likelihood of getting a ballistics report seems to be quite good.

I see at least two casings on the ground. The other or others may have rolled under the car. Not picked up. That narrows it down to a pistol. An additional fact that may come in handy at some point.

I retrieve my flashlight and look in the interior. At first glance, nothing suspicious is visible. Of course, the first officers on the scene have secured the vehicle and retrieved the gun. A detailed search, with a K-9, will be done later. I move over to the rear of the vehicle of and look at the officers. Both nod, meaning that the trunk has been checked.

I take a look at the surroundings. The street is lined with shops. All are closed now. There doesn't seem to be anyone inside any either. As I walk along the sidewalk, I notice a liquor store a hundred feet from where the shooting took place. Liquor stores are almost always equipped with a camera, both inside and outside, given that they are frequently targets of robberies or shoplifting. I make a note of the store's name.

I see John's SUV approaching, grill lights flashing. At about the same time, I see another unmarked car approach.

John gets out of his car and walks toward the scene. He stops to have a word with the patrolmen and then looks in my direction. I nod to him.

'Luc Tyler,' I say to him as he approaches.

'Drug deal gone bad?' John asks.

'An ambush, probably a supposed friend. His .38 was still behind him.'

'A possibly friendly who changed sides or a lure and kill. We'll soon find out. Probably in the next few days.'

The other unmarked car has stopped a little further ahead of John's SUV. I see Ray Stevens, Senior Detective – Vice, step out. He notices us and approaches, taking a look around.

'Luc Tyler,' he says, shaking his head.

'Turf war?' John asks.

'There's always one brewing. Lately, we had heard Luc was trying to expand, stepping on some toes in the process, some very sensitive toes.'

'Any idea about the perp then?' I inquire.

'A few come to mind. Look, it could be one his own guys trying to stop what they think are dangerous moves by Luc. They may be trying to avoid an ugly street war.'

'So, we have no eyewitnesses. Not unusual. Good place for a meet-up or ambush. It's a commercial block and unlikely anyone is working this late,' John remarks, looking down the block.

'We can start with Luc's recent skirmishes. I should have something pretty soon,' Stevens informs us.

John pops open the trunk and lifts the cover. The flashlight illuminates the corners. At the far-left corner, I see a misalignment in the upholstery. I shine my flashlight on that spot. John pulls on the false panel.

Inside the hidden compartment are two sawn-off shotguns and an Uzi-type handgun. That's enough firepower for a small gang war.

'This guy wasn't expecting a hostile reception. Otherwise, he'd have bodies holding those guns,' I remark.

'Seems that way. The way it went down, looks like an intra-gang thing,' adds John.

Stevens is on the phone with his team members or Lieutenant.

It takes around three hours by the time the ME has cleared the crime scene. The van finally leaves the scene. What was a buzzing scene of activity has now fallen silent.

John turns to Stevens.

'We will be taking this in our dossier. Hope there are no jurisdictional issues here.'

'I cleared that with the LT. From our side, we will give you the info we have. I'm a phone call away,' Stevens assures.

John looks at me.

'I'm going to start with the footage tomorrow, starting with the liquor store camera,' I give my plan of action.

Stevens nods to both of us and leaves in his car.

'So, you are going to the L'Ascension this morning?'

'Yeah. I asked Robert to join. Hopefully, we can narrow it down.'

'Talk to the uniforms about getting that footage. I don't see much hope for eyewitnesses.'

I return to my apartment. My schedule has been altered but not by much.

Some time ago, I read an article in the Times. It was written by a fellow runner who went for early morning runs in Central Park. One of the things she suggested was to sleep in your running wear so your reluctance to changing from your pajamas is not a factor. It was a real revelation for me. So, five days a week, at five am, I get up from my bed, put on my sneakers and hit the road. Five miles later, I'm back at home for the rest of my routine. After that, a nice hot shower and I'm ready to go.

With the early morning call, I grab a black coffee on my way back and then go through my morning routine. The hot shower and black coffee makes me feel that I'm on track again.

Before L'Ascension, I am stopping by the precinct. I am planning to stop by Hansie's desk before heading to my office. I need to file the report on the early morning homicide. No getting around that.

Entering my cubicle has a calming effect on me. My things are exactly where I left them. My password remains the same. The chair feels almost customized. I have just about started on the report when John pops his head in.

'Elsworth is asking to meet with us to get a status report. We need to get our ducks in a row before that.'

I nod affirmatively.

'I'll come by once I'm done with the hotel.'

The report outline is done. I'll fill in the details before leaving. Right now, I need to look up Hansie.

He is sitting in his office, his desk undecipherable. Some graphs and sketches are displayed on the screens he keeps shuttling between.

Hansie Kliepers is a South African ex-pat. A brilliant technician. With me, he has an assumption that I will discuss the latest in the cricket world every chance we get to talk, most likely given my Indian origin. Even my almost complete lack of knowledge on the subject has not convinced him to abandon the topic. But today, I need to pre-empt him before he gets carried away.

'Hey, Hansie. I need a favor from you.'

I explain to him the murder scene that I just came across. I am going to do everything I can to get to the bottom of this and try to avoid a cycle of private retribution by the parties involved.

'Got it. By the way, did you see the last Test result? South Africa won by 6 wickets and a day to spare.'

'Against who?' I regret this reflexive question as soon as it leaves my lips.

'New Zealand. You've not been following the series then?' his expression is a mix of reproach and disappointment.

'Too much going on. I will stop by later when I get a chance,' I say and make as friendly an exit as possible. Hansie is a great guy and I value the good connection we have between us.

L'Ascension

Once I have filed the report on the homicide, I walk down to the parking lot. The hotel is less than two miles away. The morning rush hour has started and it's a crawl in the downtown district. Fifteen minutes later, I am in the premises of the L'Ascension Hotel. I park my car in the visitors slot and walk to the front desk.

I identify myself to the manager and soon after I am shown to a small room marked 'Private'. Inside is a young woman, dressed in the hotel uniform. She has a large monitor in front. She looks at me as I enter with the manager.

'Sanjana, this is Detective Vilekar, KCPD. Detective, this is Sanjana, our IT specialist. She will be able to help you with your inquiry.'

Sanjana gives me a bright smile and I take my seat next to her.

'Do you want me to drive or do it yourself?' she asks me.

'I'm ok with you driving. Let's see if we can do the last six months.'

Sanjana brings up all the conferences and conventions for the last six months. The count is one-hundred-thirty-seven.

Just then there is a knock on the door. I get up from my seat and open it, to find Robert standing there.

'I'm sorry, detective, guess I didn't leave much of a margin for the rush hour.'

'We're just about getting started,' I tell him.

Narrowing down the search using the keyword 'law' reduces the number to seventeen. Further refining using additional keywords 'attorney', 'corporate', 'reform' and alternating between some other legal vocabulary takes a bit of an effort. Sanjana is smooth as silk and makes the task go faster than I would have expected. We finally settle on three conferences:

Corporate acquisitions, SPACs and role of legal counsel

Changes to tax law as related to inter-company transfer of assets

and lastly

Regional conference of corporate trial attorneys and legal advisers

Out of these three entries, the last one was the only within the last three months or so. The other two were in the five-month range.

The Regional conference was a two-day conference. The agenda had been posted online and Sanjana was able to retrieve it. The first morning had a conference and discussions scheduled in the hotel, with lunch onsite. The afternoon was at a golf club with an eighteen-hole golf course and golf lessons by a well-known pro for those who wanted to refine their swing or their putting skills, which I would think includes everyone. The dinner and stay overnight was on the club premises with a promised Las Vegas-style show.

I decide to focus on this particular event, given that the timeline is what I was looking for.

Sanjana prints out the list of participants and we start going through it.

One of the names I recognize right away:

Neil Burnham, the Senior Partner at Lambert & Burnham.

The list is pretty much a who's who of top lawyers in the city. Robert points out a name to me:

Cyril Masters

'He's Senior Counsel and Evans & Pritchard,' he informs me. I recollect that Jennifer works at the firm.

Toward the end of the list, Robert identifies someone who I think will be a good source of information.

'Michael Sutton teaches at our college,' he tells me.

'I thought this was limited to Corporate lawyers,' I say to him.

'Sutton is on the board of advisors of a couple of firms here in the city. He advises big firms on a regular basis,' Robert explains.

'That's very helpful.'

I make a note of getting an audience with Prof. Sutton at the earliest. The rest of our research does not yield anything more promising.

'I'll try to set up a meeting with Sutton today itself,' Robert says, as we walk back outdoors.

I nod appreciatively. I hope Prof. Sutton can shed some light on why the conference intrigued Tina.

Back in the precinct, I pop my head into John's office. He looks up at me inquiringly.

'Find anything useful?'

'I think so. We narrowed it down to one conference around two months ago. That looked like the best match. Robert is setting up a meeting with a professor from Gilchrist. He was there as well.'

John nods.

'Elsworth has asked me to let her know when you're back.'

'I am ready,' I answer.

Back at my desk, I am trying to find out when we can take a look at the footage of the Tyler case. I see a message from the patrol that the last 24 hours can be viewed onsite, at the store. Anything earlier will need to be ordered from the security firm that stores it in their cloud. I send back a message that I will come down and view what is available.

But first, the meeting with Elsworth.

'You have the lead on the Tyler case. But let me know if you need more boots or anything. I can get it done,' Elsworth tells us.

'I'm going down there shortly to look at the footage. So far, we have just the one store with the camera. I'm going to canvass to see if there are any others,' I offer.

'How about you, John? Between the court and the other cases you are on, are you ok?'

'I'm good so far. I've been trying to get a handle on the company finances and Tina's interactions with her brother, in particular. I think the money angle is too important to rule out.'

Elsworth nods. She looks at me.

'By the way, Hansie's got the warrant to look into the service provider's cloud. Let's see if we can find anything on the social media side.'

I give Elsworth a rundown of my work and new leads I am chasing.

'You think there was some skullduggery at that conference?'

'I'm not sure. But Tina seemed to think that and expressed that to her friends. I wouldn't want to let that slip.'

'Ok. And this person she was seeing and or helping with the drug addiction. Do we know more about that?'

'We haven't been able to track down that person so far. If she was seeing him, assuming it's a him, it was not very open or frequent. Regarding helping, I checked with the rehab centers in and around the city. I haven't seen Tina's name on any register, either as a visitor or a contact.'

Elsworth thinks for a minute. And then addresses both of us.

'There's pressure for us to get this resolved. Many out there believe this young lady was waylaid in the park while she was out for a run and it's hard to undo a belief that has taken hold. But, that said, I want to make sure we do this the right way and get the right person at the end.'

She looks at us to make sure we are with her. The message is clear: don't mess this up with impetuous actions.

'I know you are overloaded. If you need to, I can hand off the Tyler case to Burns and Ackerman. Not that they don't have their hands full, but I'm willing to work this between our teams.'

John looks at me.

'We are ok at the moment,' he informs Elsworth.

'Ok, that's great. I will leave you with it. And, by the way, if you are not getting what you need from vice, let me know. I can escalate if needed.

'One more thing: you both have worked three weekends in a row. I want you to take this weekend off, like it or not. I will not approve any overtime unless I myself call you in.'

We both nod and leave her room.

'Stevens is getting a list of suspects. I will keep you informed. But any footage is going to be key in the long run.'

'I was going to go over the footage and then canvass the neighborhood,' I tell John.

'We'll go together. My car.'

The liquor store is east off the 350 on Jarvis Street, where the shooting took place. As luck, or lack of it, would have it, there is construction work scheduled on the south side of the crime scene. The north side is still a field of grass and debris strewn about. The owner is no doubt waiting for a good price before selling it to a commercial developer. Either way, there is no camera footage for where the shooting occurred. The closest camera is to the east at the liquor store. There is no camera on the west side. John and I take a walk further down the street. There are a few stores with storefront cameras, but they are not likely to add more value than the liquor store view. Still, we will go through all information we get.

The walk-and-talk with store owners and clerks is not helpful, either.

No one was present at the time of the shooting. The liquor store owner is very helpful. He has made sure that his cameras, both inside and outside, are in good working order. He has been a victim of burglary and shoplifting once too often to be casual about it. And he will prosecute anyone trying to rob him to the fullest extent of the law, that is his promise.

To help us, he has made a copy of the footage for the last 24 hours. The 24-hour period stretches from 8am in the morning to the subsequent morning.

John and I view the footage on a small computer screen. There is nothing that looks related to the shooting, given the time frame. Looking at the footage from approximately one hour before and one hour later, there is nothing visible on the film. The implication is that both the victim and the shooter arrived from the west and the shooter exited to the west side, possibly taking the 350 or driving west on Jarvis. It is highly unlikely that either of them arrived more than one hour before the murder.

I take the usb in my possession. It will be better viewed on Hansie's workstation. And we ask the owner to order the additional footage from the security provider's cloud. There is six months in storage and we ask for all of it. It will be picked up by patrol officers as soon as it arrives.

Chapter XIV

Rohan

I am looking at the cars in the garage, trying to find one fit for the occasion. I work with my friend, Tim, souping up cars for enthusiasts. I know one speed-lover who takes his car out in the Utah desert every month, trying to set a new record. I haven't yet gone to the extent of putting a jet engine on a client's car but who knows when that day may come. That's my second job. I hesitate to call it part-time because I spend so much time with Tim. The income is not bad either. Some of our clients are willing to pay big bucks to get street-cred in the racing world.

My day job, in case you are wondering, is in network security. Now, to make a network secure, you need to know its vulnerabilities. That means trying to hack your way past whatever security has been put in place. Some of the best networks are pretty much impregnable. And that's not by accident. They have put in the dollars and the expertise, using people like me, to make sure they are not victims of a ransomware attack one fine day. Some of the companies out there, even some big, reputable ones, act like giving in to a ransomware attack on the rare occasion is preferable to putting in the resources everyday to avoid one. In my opinion, that's playing with fire.

Back to my second job, I have souped up some cars for myself. But, in the city, there's really not much you can do other than rev the engines. Street racing is a popular activity but I have mostly avoided it and ever since I met Anjie, I've moved away from it completely.

I am looking at a Honda Civic, in which I've put a 450 hp engine, with twin dual silencers. I say the roar will match any Mercedes AMG engine. There is a Chevrolet Impala that has a similar-powered engine. A few to choose from.

And there's finally the one I am going to go with. The SL 63 that I bought a few months ago. It's a smooth ride. It's got the agility to go with the looks, at least in my opinion. As I said, souping up cars for discerning clients is a nice gig. I could go full-time but I love my day job too much for that.

My good friend and colleague, Aurelien Burns, is Jordan's brother. That's how I met Anjie. Why we met is another story that I will let Anjie tell, at a time of her choosing. It's her story, more than mine. We've been together for more than a year now. I sometimes wonder at it all.

I was working in the garage late in the evening. Jordan had told me to expect a colleague from work. I was in the midst of fixing an engine issue for a client. The garage was already closed for the day. The bell rang for the side entrance. I put my tools down and went to open it. And did a double-take when I saw her.

By far the most beautiful woman I had ever seen. Anjie was dressed in a t-shirt and jeans. Her jet-black hair was loose by her shoulders. Her light brown eyes were sparkling in the light coming from the office.

'Rohan Bentan?' were the first words out of her mouth.

I nodded Yes, trying to catch my breath.

'Jordan mentioned I would be coming by?'

'Yes, she did,' I answered; my voice had come back.

'I'm Anjali Vilekar, KCPD. You can call me Anjie, if you wish.'

I took it as a good sign. We shook hands. I think I must have gotten carried away, because the next question I asked was:

'Vilekar. Sounds English. Do you have an English background?'

She looked at me for a moment.

'Can we keep the chit-chat for a little later?'

So that's what I did. The work was eyes-and-ears only. I must say I had never interacted with the police before and I was weighing my response. But given that we have just one life to live and the fact that I was being asked for help by the most beautiful woman I'd ever laid eyes on, I could hardly say no.

Once that was decided I tried the charm again.

'So, can we get back to the chit-chat now?'

Anjie gave a small smile.

'Now is ok. And to answer your question – No. I don't have any English background I know of. My dad is from a place called Goa in India and my mom is from Mumbai. They met in college.'

I nodded. Of course, I knew of both places. Who doesn't? Going to Goa someday has been on my to-do list for a while.

'What about Bentan? What's the story there?' she asked.

'Long story but I don't know it that well. My family is from Suriname. We moved here when I was a kid – three years old. Been here ever since. My dad came to work with his friend setting up a machine tool factory. It was easier then. My mom is Dutch. My dad's family are a mix of Indian, Dutch and Latin. They met when dad was studying in The Netherlands. I haven't really delved into it too much.'

Anjie seemed genuinely interested.

'Suriname, wow. I think you are the first person from Suriname I've ever met.'

'Not surprising. There's less than fifteen thousand of us here in the US. I guess people just don't want to move out as much.'

We didn't go on our first date until after the op had been completed and Anjie had recovered from the bullet wound. But she made sure I got out of it unscathed.

'I could never forgive myself if something happened to you while working for me,' she had said.

So, here I am. The SL is ready to go. I've been meaning to hang out with Anjie at my cottage (my parents' cottage actually, but they've never said no to me, ever) for the last two months but Anjie has always had something come up at the last minute. That's the job, that's who she is. The fact is, if it wasn't her job, we would never have met. I'm just so happy that we could make it today.

The cottage is really nice, with a private lake and a bonfire pit. I think it will be good for her to get away from it all for a weekend. And I know it will be great for me to get some exclusive time with her. Anjie likes biking, hiking, fishing, camping out. all outdoor activities. For that, I've got all the gear we will need, at the cabin. My hope is that Anjie will have a good time.

Chapter XV

Anjie

A weekend *décontracté* (or is it?)

It feels so good to be sleep in once in a while instead of waking up with the alarm at five am. The last few days have been hectic, to say the least. I don't have a problem working weekends or even going without sleep for days on end. But there comes a time when you hit the law of diminishing returns. Your mind gets saturated. And I have a feeling that Elsworth has that intuition to not let it get to that point.

I have to be honest. If Elsworth hadn't forced a weekend break, I would be at the office trying to chase leads down. But now that there's no choice, I'm really looking forward to some time with Rohan at his cottage. I've been there before with him and I found it a very nice place. There are some great trails for hiking or biking. I think it's a great day for a hike today. I've packed my hiking boots and gear. Rohan is good with the supplies part of things. I don't have to worry about that. For me, it's the boots, the bug spray that I need to make sure of.

I'm not doing my morning run today. I reckon I can get enough activity with a good, long hike. I go through the stretching and yoga and then, a nice hot shower to get the day started. Just about ready at the agreed time.

I get a text from Rohan. He is downstairs in the parking lot. I grab my bag and head out. Mei is still sleeping. I've already let her know my plans, as I have to John and Elsworth. They need to know who is available to attend, when.

I see Rohan in the visitors' spot, with his Benz. When I first met him, I had no idea how lucrative this whole business is. What I like is that he loves working with cars. It's his passion, right next to his love of software. And no, I wouldn't want him to work with my dad.

I smile when I see him. I can't help smiling. I am always happy when I see him. I think that may be because he is always happy to see me. His smile is natural, it's with his whole being; his eyes and his entire manner.

He gives me a kiss.

'You look absolutely stunning!' he says. And I know he means it.

I laugh.

'Really? Not bad, yourself.'

It's a nice, warm day. A little breeze. I hope it won't get too hot. Right now, it's perfect.

We get started. It's too early in the morning for a lot of traffic. For the weekend, that is. It's a fairly smooth ride out of the city and on the open road. The drive is about two hours.

I reach out and touch Rohan's arm and gently caress it. He looks at me and smiles. He takes my hand in his and gently squeezes it.

'It's so good to see you get some time for yourself,' he says.

'I've been looking forward to this,' I whisper.

Rohan looks at me and strokes my arm with the back of his hand. And smiles. Then he brushes my hair back from my face. It doesn't help. The wind is going to keep blowing it back and forth. We are driving with the top down.

He is patient generally and that carries through in the driving. Of course, he knows it would be embarrassing, for him and me, to be caught speeding or something else, while I am with him. But the road is mostly clear and we cruise along nicely.

The cabin is on a hill. The path is winding, with a scenic view all around. I take in the scenery. It's breathtaking, really. I am always overcome with a sense of perspective when looking at the vastness of nature all around. As in, are we really as significant as we presume ourselves to be?

Rohan opens the wrought iron gate. The driveway is lined with river rocks which crunch under the tires as we park in front of the entrance doors. I've been here before but it's been a while. Rohan gets the stuff from the car. It's not much, just some of my personal items and his. The place is going to be well-stocked. Rohan closes the door behind him and looks at me.

'There, all set. What do you want to do?' he asks.

'Well, first things first,' I answer.

We are both standing in the middle of the foyer. I take a step toward him. He moves toward me and takes my hands in his.

'You're so beautiful,' he says.

Our lips meet, slowly, really slowly. Take the time when you have it. Still, I can't believe the slow pace Rohan is on. Even after knowing him for more than a year.

Slowly, he starts to unbutton my top, each button interspersed with a slow kiss.

'Are you playing Despacito in your head?' I ask.

'Patience, love. I've waited two months for this. I am enjoying the moment,' he answers.

The problem is, I don't think my patience is going to last. I gasp when he moves his mouth all over. Kissing everywhere. I get his clothes off and what was remaining of mine.

We are on the bed. Rohan has really decided to stick with his cadence; my impatience does not seem to have had much of an effect. He is moving his mouth from my forehead down now, redoing his routine when he was removing my blouse. But now, he is using his hands at the same time, moving slowly, so slowly, that my movements cannot match. Involuntarily, I start moving faster. Rohan's rhythm remains the same, proceeding all the way down, where he lingers for a really long time, until I can't take it anymore. I pull him close to me.

Rohan has prepared coffee for us that we are having in bed. A couple of cups later, we are ready to head out. I have my hiking boots and outfit on, as does Rohan. The weather is darn near perfect. We decide to go to one of the hiking trails nearby. It's a great trail, with some varieties of birds that you rarely get to see. There is some dampness in the ground, caused by the rain overnight. The trail we have taken is around ten miles. On the way we meet some fellow hikers. This trail isn't that crowded, which is one of the things I like about it.

We have some canteen with us. Water and sandwiches. We are walking, holding hands and making out from time to time. This is going to be a long hike, can't go by miles per hour. The ten miles takes about twice the time as would take for a straightforward hike, but it's been more than twice as enjoyable. The sun is low on the horizon. I can feel the slight chill of the evening air just about starting. By the time we are back, our sandwiches are done. We are both in a mood for a hot meal. We head out to a small diner in one of the strip malls a couple of miles away.

The pizza is really good. We have ordered a large Mediterranean between the two of us. We are in the middle of it when I notice something in the parking lot.

What draws my attention is an ongoing interaction between a couple. Both look to be in their early twenties. From what I can see, there is some argument going and the young man is trying to get his partner – most likely his girlfriend – in the car. But the young woman is not of the same mind. On two occasions that I notice, the man has grabbed the woman by the arm to get her in the car. And she has jerked her arm away both times.

The light is getting rather low. From my backpack, I grab the Glock and shove it in my waistband. I string my shield around my neck. The better for it to be visible right away.

'I'll be right back,' I say to Rohan, interrupting our conversation.

He is a little surprised and says nothing.

I walk out to the parking lot and slowly approach the couple.

I show my badge and identify myself.

'Detective Vilekar, KCPD. Is there a problem here?' I ask.

I am about ten yards away. I have no intention of drawing the gun unless I see no other alternative.

'No problem, officer. We are just about to go home,' says the young man.

I look at the man and then at the woman. I get the feeling that the woman wants to say something but is not sure that she should.

'How about you, ma'am. Do you want to go home with him?' I address her.

The woman looks to be at a loss for words. The man has grown increasingly impatient.

'Get in the car, Cindy,' he says gruffly, his hand on her shoulder, pressuring her into the passenger seat.

'Hold on, sir. I need to hear from the lady,' I say firmly.

I am now within around six feet of the couple. The man shoves the woman once more, this time so forcefully that she hits her head on the door frame.

'Get in,' he orders.

I intervene, I have to at this point.

'Step back, sir. I am placing you under arrest for assault. Please put your hands on the hood of the car and spread your legs shoulder width apart.'

'Just mind your own goddamn business, fucking sp*c bitch,' he retorts.

I am hoping and praying the situation doesn't escalate, that I won't need to draw my weapon. All I have is my .40 caliber Glock. No taser.

I try to make my voice sound as calm as possible. And I don't give any weight to the slur he has directed towards me.

'Please do as I ask, sir. I want all of us to be safe and secure.'

The young man gives me a sullen look but does as asked. I step forward to search his person for weapons. My hand is hovering on my Glock as I approach, but I necessarily have to have both hands in front for the search. I am now right behind him and start to pat him. The moment my hands make contact, he turns around and aims a right hook at my jaw.

This is a fraught moment, always is. When an officer tries to place a person under arrest. But, I've practiced his particular procedure and this reaction hundreds of times with Jordan and other officers in my precinct. I step back and almost completely avoid the blow. But he does graze my chin. This is the moment. His weight is completely on his left foot with his turning motion. I step forward with my left foot and with my right, I sweep his left foot off the floor. This sends him crashing to the ground. Before he can turn around, I have my knee on his back and I slip a pair of zip ties over his wrists.

Yes, I know what you may ask. The answer is: I am supposed to carry my service weapon and the means to secure a prisoner at all times.

I then complete the search I had started, for any weapons. There are none. I retrieve his wallet. He has a local address. I run his driver's license and find no record. But now, in addition to the assault I observed, I have assault on an officer and resisting arrest. I say a prayer of thanks internally that I did not need to use deadly force.

I look at the young lady. She hasn't spoken up all this time. I turn to her.

'Do you have family nearby?'

'Yes,' she nods.

'I would suggest you ask them to fetch you. In case you need assistance, please get in touch with me.'

I give her my card with my contact information.

I ask for officer assistance for processing the arrest. Within a few minutes, a patrol car arrives on the scene. The whole procedure, including a medical check for me and my sworn affidavit, takes long enough that the sun has set by the time I am back at the cottage. The patrol officer drops me off on the porch.

'Have a good evening detective, I hope you can enjoy the rest of the weekend.'

I nod a thanks.

The adrenalin that was pumping has now given way to a tiredness, a culmination of all the day's events. Now that I have time to think, the same kind of thoughts go through my mind that have gone through before, the time I was shot during an operation. This injury is far less serious. I am not sure what department procedures will apply.

Could the events have unfolded differently? Why did I intervene in the dispute to begin with? What if I had needed to use deadly force? It could have happened, if the blow had connected to my jaw with full impact and I was the ground, I would have been compelled to draw my gun. And then, all bets are off. Once you draw it, you are prepared to fire.

My reason for intervening was very clear. I fully believed that the woman was in danger and if the man had forced the woman in the vehicle, the likelihood of something terrible happening was very high. No doubt in my mind.

I have already noted down the woman's contact information and I will follow up with her in the near future.

'You ok?' Rohan asks.

'I will be,' I answer.

He has made pasta with chicken and Alfredo sauce. It's pretty good, but I pick at my food. My appetite is not there. I leave my plate on the table and go for a shower. The hot water is soothing. I come out of the shower and go straight to bed. I think I am asleep before I even pull the duvet over me.

Chapter XVI

Anjie

Back to work

I am back here at my desk. It's sixty-thirty am on Monday morning. The weekend was a real I-don't-know-what-to-say. I went down to the precinct again on Sunday. The sergeant told me he had checked on Cindy and that she was with her family. Turns out she was the man's girlfriend and they had just moved in together.

Cindy is not sure that she will press charges for the assault. But there is still time to decide that. I wondered what would have happened if I hadn't intervened when I did. Counterfactuals are always difficult. But it is worthwhile noting that abuse escalates if left unchecked.

This morning, I am meeting with Michael Sutton, the professor at Gilchrist. Robert has obtained an appointment for the morning. In the meantime, I am looking at the footage from the Luke Tyler scene.

Here is the thing. I see no one casing the location, not immediately before the shooting. It's a happy coincidence for the shooter that there were no surveillance cameras that caught them in the act. But was it a happy coincidence/luck? Or did they know the spot beforehand. That takes it from spontaneous to pre-meditated. I still need to get more evidence and information regarding the circumstances. But trying to decipher the evidence we have in hand is likely to help us in our search.

I decide to stop by Hansie's desk. It's now almost seventy-thirty. I know he comes in early. Sure enough, he is at his desk, looking at camera footage on his screen. He looks up when I knock.

'Anji, I heard about your encounter. Are you ok?'

'I am fine. Just a small bruise.'

'Elsworth call you?'

'Yes, she did. So did Roman. I think I may have to go for a session with the therapist.'

Elsworth called me later that evening after that incident in the parking lot. She was concerned for me and I got the impression that I may have to spend some time with the therapist for dealing with PTSD. Guidelines have changed in recent years. Even a minor injury is treated seriously. The thinking being that untreated mental ailments will have a growing deleterious impact on job performance.

'Has the footage come in from the Tyler case?' I ask.

'Not yet. I am expecting that by today evening. I will be working on Tina's phone this morning and the social media accounts. Her phone has few records, just a couple days worth. But I will be looking at the cloud to see if I can find anything. The service providers have given me access after I got the warrant.'

'Ok, thanks, keep me posted.'

'Will do,' Hansie signs off with a smile.

John is on the phone with someone when I knock on his door. He looks at me and signals me to wait. He hangs up shortly after.

'Vilekar, I see you're up and early.'

'Yeah, I want to get an early start.'

'Eventful weekend. Hope you are ok.'

'I'm ok. Glancing blow.'

'That's fortunate. These things can escalate fairly quickly.'

'I was lucky to be there to intervene. I hope Cindy will be ok. Gotta meet with Elsworth as well.'

Roman nods.

'I am planning to go to Gilchrist this morning, after meeting with Elsworth,' I add.

'Let's go in my car.'

I nod. I question whether John is saying that to save me the driving. I'm not that worried about the wound. Departmental procedures are another matter. I wonder what Elsworth has in store for me. I walk over to her cabin and she motions me in.

'Detective, I hope you are doing well.'

I assure her that I am.

'I wanted to let you know that I spoke with the Sergeant over there. He assured me that it's a clear-cut case. The lady in question gave a statement that indeed she was assaulted and in plain sight. She hasn't yet decided on pressing charges. Your intervention was fully justified.'

I feel a sense of relief. Even though my mind was clear on that, to hear it officially is comforting.

'Glad to hear it,' I respond.

'Well, you still have to attend the therapist session. I would like you to schedule one this week. If you have difficulty getting a slot, let me know.'

I respond Yes.

I am just about to leave for my meeting with Prof. Sutton when Jordan knocks. She gives me a hug. I am really glad to have a friend like Jordan. I know she has my back when I need it, just like I have hers.

'You may have saved that girl's life,' she says to me.

'Didn't look good the way it was going,' I tell her.

We chat for a bit and agree to meet for a drink.

When John and I arrive at Sutton's office, we find him in a discussion with a student. He quickly finishes and lets us in.

We introduce ourselves.

'You are here about the conference I attended in the city?'

'That's correct. We would like to know more about it.'

Prof. Sutton appears to be a bit on the defensive.

'Look,' he says, 'that was a very useful conference, with some of the best in the field.'

'We wanted to know more about the golf outing and the evening that followed,' I ask.

'The golf outing was a mini tournament. The prize was just a token. I think it was a trip for two to Disneyworld. No, what it was really was a bunch of rich folks trying to outdo each other, any way they could. I was paired with a retired professor, who I know well.'

'How did you do, then?' John asks.

'Myself, not too well. I finished 7 over. My partner finished 5 over. There were some good players out there.'

'And after the golfing, I believe you had a dinner with some show planned?'

'There was a show, some singers and a couple of dance performances, the kind you see on the talent shows on TV. I must say they were very good.'

'Professor, I need to ask you about the hostesses that were present during the dinner. Did you notice anything, specifically in terms of hooking up?' I ask.

'I thought you would ask about that. There were ladies present and they were there to keep you company for the dinner, even getting drinks etc. I didn't really delve into it. A couple of them stopped by my side – the dinner was a standing up affair to facilitate mingling – and offered to keep me company. Even though they didn't come out and say anything explicitly, I had the feeling that things might go further if I wanted them to. I politely brushed it aside.'

'Anything you noticed among the other guests?'

'I did see some of the guests chatting with the ladies. What transpired after, I am not sure. If there were any liaisons, I assume they were discreetly arranged.'

'After the dinner and show, did you stay overnight at the club or did you go back to the hotel?'

'I went back to the hotel myself. There were some people who stayed here overnight. The charges for a room were very nominal, I think. I had no intention of spending out-of-pocket and anyway, I had all of my personal items back at the hotel. So, after the evening concluded, the organizers arranged for a car to transport me back.'

John and I thank the professor and step outside.

'I can't believe there would be no hanky-panky going on if it went like the professor described,' I say to John.

John nods.

'I think the question is whose hanky-panky are we after. And then, did it go on at the club or at the hotel,' John is thinking aloud.

'Neil Burnham is an obvious choice for us. And Jennifer Adams works at Evans & Pritchard. I would say we start with this.'

John agrees with me. We decide to follow up with canvassing of both sites: the hotel and the golf club.

Time flies on Monday and before I know it, it's lunch time. I have no time for an elaborate lunch. I grab the sandwich that I packed at my apartment and walk down to Hansie's desk. His text earlier said that he had something that could be worth looking into.

When I walk in, I find Hansie with his feet on his desk, leaning back and biting into a sub. I can't decipher exactly what the filling is.

On the monitor in front of him is a cricket match. The stadium seems to be completely packed and I suppose there is a lot of noise, but I can't hear any of it, with Hansie using his noise cancelling headphones.

I tap him on the shoulder and he looks up at me, as if in surprise. Then he hits pause on the video and takes off his headphones. I take the opportunity to pull up a chair and start on my sandwich.

'Shit, Anjie, I was just getting to the last two overs,' he says, almost reproachfully.

'It's still there waiting for you, after I'm gone,' I reply, with a dry tone.

He grins.

'Ok, I got something from Tina's phone, her social media.'

He grabs a printout from his desk and glances over it.

'The social media is almost all very innocuous. Except for one particular back and forth. Now, I have gone back on the cloud for about three months. Everything before that has been purged. I think that's because Tina was running out of space here as well and so she had set an automatic purging program. Even so, I found some messages in this period. There were five in total, four from the person to Tina and one back from

Tina saying that she does not wish to communicate further. Not many. But the person was repeatedly trying to get Tina to get into a relationship. Tina did not seem all that interested.'

He hands me a printout which contain the messages he's been able to retrieve.

'Do we know who was sending these?'

'The account is not verified. But it's a person for sure. I don't have a name but I do have a location.'

He looks on his screen, then at me.

'The messages, all of them, originated from a location downtown. I checked the IP with the provider. This is a small place, a coffee shop. They have good wifi, which attracts a few regulars who work on their laptops.'

I look at the name of the shop he has on the screen. I know this place. A popular place with good coffee. I have picked up a cup and a muffin from there myself on occasion.

'Has there been any activity recently, after the homicide?'

'I haven't seen any messages since. Although, there is ongoing activity at the location with the IP. Mainly browsing and email. Looks like he or she are in there weekday evenings.'

I switch to another topic.

'Where are we with the Tyler footage?'

'Gonna get to it. I should have that, at least the last two weeks, in a couple of days.'

'I need to know if anyone was casing the neighborhood. I don't think this rendezvous was set up spontaneously.'

'Yeah, ok. Anything suspicious, then. Got it.'

I finish my sandwich and get up to leave. Hansie is already into the last over of the cricket match as I exit his office.

Chapter XVII

Anjie

What's Reilly up to?

The downtown area is humming with activity in certain parts at this time in the late evening. The offices have long since closed but the bars and nightclubs are just about getting in the swing of things.

TJ's is a popular bar and nightclub. It attracts all kinds of clientele, from college kids to office executives. Needless to say, there is a strong presence of the unsavory here as well. The kind selling all kinds of stuff to the well-heeled.

I spot Reilly at one of the tables where he is joking and swigging on an IPA with some folks who look to be barely out of high school. John has followed me from the other side of the room and knows I have spotted our target. We both close in on Reilly at the same time. Luckily, he is there by himself, without his usual sidekicks. Reilly is a harmless miscreant but has a soft spot for stealing smartphones. His m.o. is to steal phones and then sell them to customers at a discount, along with pre-paid sims. He is usually smart enough to discard the stolen sims and smart enough to delete find-my-phone apps.

Reilly notices me as I approach and his first thought is making a getaway. But John has blocked the escape route on the other side. Reilly changes his demeanor from fugitive to jovial.

'Reilly, how are you doing?' John addresses him, in the manner of an old acquaintance.

'I'm good. How can I help you, bro?' Reilly quips back.

I do not want to humiliate Reilly in front of his friends. We need his cooperation, though. Reilly accompanies us outside on the street.

'We're trying to trace a number, a burner,' I tell him.

I show him the number that Tina got a call from the evening of her death.

Reilly looks at it for a moment and then shakes his head.

'Can't say for sure. Not in the latest batch I sold, at least. I'll take a look and ask around.'

I supply him the other numbers that Tina had received calls from, calls made from burners in the days before. Reilly promises to get on it.

'I need that yesterday,' I say to him. Reilly nods in understating. Homicide detectives don't ask for help unless there is a homicide connected.

The coffee shop with free wi-fi

It's the fourth evening in a row that I am sitting in front of the coffee shop, actually a little distance from the entrance, so as not to be conspicuous. With my camera, I am taking pictures of everyone who goes in and comes out. Jordan is beside me. This is a low-risk stakeout, but even so, I have a partner in case things go south.

After each shift, I go to the lab and run a face recognition program against the photos I have taken. That database only contains those with a criminal record. But still, that's something. So far, I have come across five people in the database, none of whom look likely to be candidates for stalking Tina.

The coffee shop does not have surveillance cameras. The only way to identify anyone is to get the footage ourselves.

'Maybe the guy stopped coming by?' Jordan asks me, looking up from the computer screen.

'Maybe. I still need to keep going for a while. He could be taking a break from his routine.'

I am certain that the person is male. As is Jordan. I figure I need to do this for a week before thinking about taking a break. After all, it could be the fellow has given up on this particular café.

'So, how are things working out with Rohan?' Jordan asks.

'As good as these things can go. He is patient but I'm not sure how many times he can stand having plans cancelled before he decides it's too much,' I reply.

I guess there is a tinge of melancholy in my voice and Jordan is too sharp not to notice.

'Don't get down, babe. From what I hear, he's head over heels.'

I nod absent-mindedly. It's good to hear that, but then, what would you expect him to say? It's not like we're having problems, but after my previous experiences, I don't take anything for granted.

It's now close to seven-thirty. Only a half hour to go before the shop closes. I've almost resigned myself to repeating this another day. That's when I see this figure in a black hoodie walking toward the entrance. The pace is not too brisk but still lively. I raise my camera lens and point it, to find Prof Nunes squarely in my sights. I gasp audibly and Jordan looks at me. I take the pictures as he enters the store and then look at her.

'That's Nunes, Tina's professor and former advisor. I half expected an older male here but it's still shocking.'

Jordan shakes her head.

'You just can't rule anyone out,' she opines.

We wait outside, still keeping an eye for any further customers. After around forty-five minutes, Nunes leaves the café. The way his appearance is, he could have been out for a run and just dropped in for a drink. I will need to speak with the owners to verify if he is a regular customer.

At eight o'clock the café sign is turned to Closed. Jordan and I wait for a couple of minutes and then make our way to the door. I knock a couple of times. A young woman opens it and looks at us quizzically. We display our badges. She opens the door to let us in.

Inside, there is a middle-aged lady working on the cash register and making entries in a journal. I assume this to be the owner. She looks at me with some alarm in her eyes. I will need to do my best to put her at ease.

'Good evening, ma'am. Are you the owner of this store?' I ask.

'Yes, I am. How can I help you?' she answers.

John and I decided early on not to let on that her store would be under surveillance. That's to avoid any giveaways to customers by a change in behavior. But now, with Nunes, I am as certain as I can be that we have our suspect.

On my phone, I show her the photograph of Nunes that I have just snapped. She looks at it for a couple of seconds and then looks up at me in surprise.

'He was just in here. Have you been watching our store?' her demeanor is slightly ruffled.

'We are working on a case. I would request you to keep this confidential. And please be assured, neither you nor your business are in any sort of trouble.'

The owner assures us that she will not mention our presence.

'He's a regular customer here, although I haven't seen him in a few weeks. He usually comes here with his laptop and sometimes he's here for an hour or more. He usually orders quite a few items. Unlike some others who order a cup of coffee and occupy a table for half a day. I don't usually mind people taking their time, but at busy times, I really wish they would be more considerate.'

I thank the lady and we leave the store.

'What now?' Jordan asks.

'I think this is it. He's the one we are after, as far as the solicitation goes. I hope the lady keeps her word about us. What I'm thinking is we need to get some background information on this guy before confronting him. If he was sending messages to Tina, it's more than likely he was sending similar stuff to other students.'

Jordan nods in agreement.

'Pathological behavior. I'm pretty sure there are others.'

Luc Tyler

I'm walking to John's desk when I see someone knocking on his entrance. Its Ray Stevens, Detective, Vice, standing there, a cup of coffee in his hand. In the other hand is a tray with two Starbucks cups, Grande size. He sees me and nods in greeting.

'Thought I'd drop by to give you the latest on Luc Tyler. You know, the dealer that got shot,' he says, adding the context in case the matter had faded from our memory.

'Not sure if you guys were in need of one or not,' he forwards the tray toward John and I. I grab one, I could really use it about now. John says a no thanks.

'No problem, I'm sure there will be a taker or two,' Stevens quips, with a smile.

'What you got for us?' John asks.

'I've been talking to some sources on the street. There isn't a turf war brewing, at least not right now. So, it could just be a deal gone bad.'

'That's comforting. We'll be taking a look at some earlier footage to see if we can spot anyone casing the neighborhood. We'll keep you informed,' John informs Stevens.

'Great. And I'll let you guys know if we hear anything as well.'

Stevens smiles and leaves.

'I've had one cup too many already,' John says to me.

I nod. I've already informed John about Nunes being the stalking suspect. I am here to discuss how we go after him.

'I think we need to spread the net for more victims. I'm sure he has done this more than once. I confirmed with Hansie that the account belongs to him. The problem is that he's been cleaning up his account so as not to leave traces behind. There's some criminal expertise there, makes our task no easier,' I suggest.

'There may be similar messages to other students. Even if he's purged his account, we may be able to track down someone who had that experience.'

'The way I was thinking to go about it, I am going to look at transcripts of students who took his classes. We may find a suspicious pattern.'

'That and his movements on the day, if we can trace them. A bit premature to ask him for an alibi at the moment, but we can lay the groundwork.'

A forensic audit

John and I are at the offices of Kevin Esselstein, the Forensic Auditor. Esselstein works for a well-known auditing firm and has done forensics audits for the KCPD in some high-profile cases.

'Mr. Esselstein, how are you doing? Detective Roman and this is my partner, Detective Vilekar,' John makes the introductions.

'Oh, please, it's Kevin,' Esselstein says, shaking our hands with a firm grip. 'Give me a minute here. I've been looking at this material just to refresh my memory on some of the key details.'

He has the reports in front of him and is cross-checking on his computer. He addresses us once he is done.

'I've been going over this the last weeks. It's not a large-scale fraud. But there are definitely signs of some questionable transactions. I would say that further investigation will make things clearer. If we are talking about a full-scale audit, that would be a wide-ranging and costly exercise.'

'So, what are we talking about? Phony accounts, skimming?' John asks.

'Let me explain. What am seeing is payments make to different business entities for consulting fees. Now, consulting fees are commonplace and perfectly legitimate. You can think of any of the big consulting firms offering such services. Here, the consulting fees have gone to businesses, some of whom are well-known and others that are not so well-known. I have here a list of such payments over the last five years.'

'There are overall eleven different business over the last five years that have received such payments. I conducted preliminary checks of the businesses, some appear to be legitimate, with websites and all. But I haven't been able to establish a record, at least I couldn't find anything substantial after a brief check. The thing is, there are new businesses popping up all the time, some of them go on to be multi-billion dollar companies. So, I am not questioning the legitimacy of all the businesses. But it is worth looking into, all the same.'

'If we start looking at the last year, do you see anything suspicious?' I ask. Reverse chronological order is what I will need to concentrate my energy on.

Esselstein, or Kevin, looks back at his large monitor for a minute or so.

'In the last year, there have been regular payments to three businesses. The main function of two of these businesses is stated as improved marketing strategies. The third business is listed as a customer relationship management business. The total payout to these three firms in the last year was about a half-million dollars. I can give you the specifics right now.'

Kevin sends a command on his monitor and the laser printer starts printing. He collects the pages and hands a copy to each of us. There are four pages, printed double-sided – the environmentally friendly method.

I look down at my copy. There is a list of the businesses, with the names and the websites associated. All three have individual websites – a common practice nowadays. The listed entries are the amounts and dates of each particular transaction related to the payments. The banks listed alongside are located within the city.

Two of the three businesses have accounts in the same bank. That will make my life that much easier.

'I have printed out the questionable transactions for each year,' he informs us, handing over additional printed copies.

'Is there enough here to request a formal audit?' John asks.

'In my opinion, no. This is a privately-held company. If it was public, there would be a public interest factor in requesting a complete audit. Here, we don't have enough evidence of wrong-doing. And even if we did obtain such evidence, it would need to be at a scale where you had significant malfeasance, for example, to evade taxes or establish breach of trust. I don't think we're there yet.'

John and I go over the papers, peppering Esselstein with additional questions. I must say, he is a patient soul. He answers with clarity and explains to us some of the salient points he has observed. We thank him and leave his office.

'Well, that was an informative session,' John looks at me.

'Seems to me that owning a private company gives one more of a leeway,' I retort.

I am well aware that my father's company is privately owned. However, I am quite sure that he would notice anything amiss and I can't even dream he would try any shenanigans with a business he toiled days and nights, years on end, building. That's why every year, he has a reputed auditing firm go through his company finances, with a fine-tooth comb.

'Looks like a double-edged sword. If they don't catch the malfeasance in time, it could become far worse a situation with the passage of time. To some extent, I think every company depends on the integrity of its officers and employees.'

'The banks are going to be cagey about giving us details of their customers' accounts,' I turn to the task now awaiting us.

'We have a partial subpoena for matters related to this homicide. If the bank is going to play tough, we can get a court order. It may take some time but they know it will be inevitable.'

I nod in assent. It's better to try the friendly approach to begin with.

Chapter XVIII

Anjie

Marty Danton

The street is rather quiet. There are a couple of women carrying what look to be sacks of groceries. One of them is using a two-wheeled cart that has a bag you can put your stuff in. The other woman is carrying two bags, one in each hand. As our car glides gently, almost noiselessly, down the path, I notice that some of the houses look like they have been abandoned. It's a bit of a hard-luck part of town here. The folks who still are here are hardworking, some of them retired after a lifetime of careers in factories or assembly lines.

The sub-prime mortgage crisis hit this part of town particularly hard. Many of the borrowers found themselves underwater, unable to make their monthly payments or sell their properties for enough to pay off what they owed. As a result, their homes were foreclosed. Some of the foreclosed homes were sold by the banks for pennies on the dollar. Investors hoping for a quick flip rushed to the scene. Some did have success. For the most part, though, they did not find any takers. Most of the businesses and stores had left. There just wasn't enough of a clientele to keep them afloat. After an initial period of success, the investors found that the effort and time was not giving them the results that they were seeking and so, many of the houses remained unoccupied.

I stop the car at the corner of Holbeck Street. John and I get out. I take a 360 look and then cross the street at the two-storey home, which is where we are headed.

The house itself is nondescript. A sky-blue exterior, a small porch and a single car garage. We approach slowly. The thing that stands out about this house is that it is completely unnoticeable from the outside. You wouldn't give it a second look if you happened to pass by it. We are here because one of our CIs has given us some information that needs to be taken care of right away.

I approach the front door. John and I are both lined up on either side. There is no movement or any sound on the inside. I look and John and gently turn the doorknob. My right hand is on my Glock, still holstered. The door opens and John steps inside. I follow a step behind.

The main floor is now visible. It is a far cry from neat and tidy. Dishes and forks are lying on the coffee table in the living room. John and I take a quick look into the nooks and crannies before signaling that there is no one on the main floor.

We make our way upstairs. John and I both are ready with our guns by our sides. This place is known to police as a drug den. But over the years, there has been no real violent criminal activity. Rather it is a place where drug users have found a safe haven. In addition, there is a usually someone with Narcan on the premises. I would confidently say that quick administration of Narcan has saved many a life over the years in this place.

I am looking for Marty Danton. For some reason, Marty has decided to show up in this house. Perhaps it is to check whether everything is ok. Marty is a member of the Tyler gang, the same Luc Tyler whose murder cut his own reign short. Marty was one of his assistants, way down the ladder, more of an errand-boy. After Tyler's death, his status in the hierarchy is probably being determined. I guess it would depend on who finally takes over the reins. I am hoping Marty may have heard something. Something useful that may point us in the right direction. If Stevens's information is correct and the hit was an inside job, Marty may have some useful information. When my CI called to say Marty was in this location, it seemed too good an opportunity to let go.

The second floor is a four-bedroom unit. We check two bedrooms. The first room door we open has three young adults who look to be barely out of their teens. There are no beds here, just mattresses laid out on the floor. Two of the young men are asleep while the young woman is propped up against the wall. She gives me a blank stare before looking away. I take a quick look around and then close the door behind. The second room is similar to the one I just looked through. But in here, there are two middle-aged ladies and a man who looks to be around sixty-five. His skin is sallow and wrinkled, making him appear a lot older than he is and frail enough. The folks are either asleep or in a state of stupor from injecting themselves. That is one reason we have not gone in guns blazing. The other reason, strange as it may sound, is that this is an firearms-free zone. The house, that is. This is to avoid unintended catastrophe. The combination of drugs and guns is never a good idea.

In the third bedroom we open the door to, I see Marty. He is talking on the phone animatedly. He looks up and recognizes us. Of course he knows who we are. Not the first time we've met. That's his bread and butter, his key to survival. He gives us a wry smile and puts up his hands. Even though we are confident he is unarmed, I give him a quick pat-down. He's clean.

While I stay with Marty, John searches the remaining parts of the second floor to ensure there is no potential danger.

John is back after his check. He looks at Marty with a quizzical eye.

'Well, well, Marty, fancy meeting you here,' he says.

'Detectives, if I had known I would be running into you, I'd have brought some donuts and coffee,' Marty retorts, with a wide grin signifying his dry humor.

'Too bad you didn't,' I say. 'Now, how come you landed up here, what's going on?'

Marty thinks for a few seconds, perhaps weighing whether to blurt out the real reason or come up with a cock-and-bull tale. Finally, it looks like he's made up his mind.

'Look, there was an issue with one of the users here. They got some stuff off the street and it was mixed up with fentanyl. The guy is okay once we gave the Narcan. I don't normally stop by. This is a self-run facility by the users but we don't want any tragedies here like the one that happened a while ago.'

I recollect the drug death that he is talking about. It was a young man, in one of the houses like this one. He had obtained his supply on the street and od'd. Unfortunately, the Narcan wasn't available to be administered on time. The paramedics had declared him dead at the scene.

'Is the guy still here?' John follows up.

'No, this was a while ago. He was taken to hospital once he recovered. I just came by to make sure none of that stuff was lying around. We don't want anyone else just pocketing it.'

Marty's story looks to be quite straight.

'So, Marty, what's going on with you now, with Luc gone?' I ask him.

Marty shakes his head. His emotion is showing. He answers after a moment of reflection.

'I don't know. I'm just trying to keep doing my regular job. You know, keeping things clean. I don't like these people trying to make a quick buck by selling all this bullshit. But I don't know how things are going to turn out.'

'Who's running things now?'

'Ganzo has taken over. He's been the second-in-command for a while now.'

'You mean Dyson Thibodeaux? Is he looking for some payback?'

Dyson, street name Ganzo, has been Luc's right-hand man for a long while.

'Of course he's gonna look for payback. This is the street, sweetie. It you aint paying back, you gonna be in line next,' Marty answers. I ignore his 'sweetie', I've been called all sorts of names on the street, as you have already seen.

'So, who had the beef, then?' John pursues.

'No idea. Look, from my viewpoint, I'm lying low, attending to business. If business dries up, we're all fucked, anyway.'

'Did Luc rub anyone the wrong way recently?'

I am trying to be persistent now that I have Marty in a relatively relaxed situation. If we get him down to the station, the whole world will know and he is more than likely to clam up.

'Listen, I haven't heard anything about that. If he did, it didn't get to me.'

Marty looks like he is being straight. I look at John and he nods to me, indicating that we can let him go. I hand him my card. One with a phony name and occupation.

'You can go, Marty. Keep your ear to the ground. If you hear anything, you have my number.'

Marty looks at the card.

'Cleanup services. That's a good one. I'll keep it in my wallet at all times.'

He gives us a sardonic smile and a fake salute and walks out. John and I are left in the house now, along with the other silent inhabitants sprawled in stupor.

'I think we can give them a check before leaving,' I suggest to John.

The fact is, there is no justification for any police action here. They are all here voluntarily. Arresting them is not an option.

We split up the rooms between us. I look at each one's pupils to check for signs of an overdose. I check the breathing as well.

When the check is completed, we walk out of the gloomy building, back into the sunshine. The scene inside the house has had an effect on me. Not just the gloom but the abjectness and the human misery. It's a shame that people who are in the throes of addiction do not have a better place to fulfil their cravings than this. I wish this city would recognize the helpless nature of addiction and give its affected citizens the support needed. A few years ago, I was in Toronto, the biggest city in our northern neighbor. There were safe places for addicts right in the middle of the downtown precinct. In Dundas square. Some tourists were perhaps bothered by it all but, in retrospect, I find the approach truer. A way to tackle reality head-on as opposed to dusting it away to a dark corner and hoping it all goes away, or at least no one notices.

'If Dyson has taken over, we can definitely expect some payback. May be a good idea to ask Stevens to keep an eye on things,' I am thinking out loud.

'What I was thinking myself. I'll reach out to him. Preferably keep things from getting out of hand.'

Dyson Thibodeaux

Dyson is a hard man to track down. I manage to get him on the phone, through intermediaries, finally. He agrees to come down to the station.

'I need to get my security detail with me,' he puts it to me as a pre-condition.

'As long as they stay off the precinct premises and don't carry illegal weapons,' I respond to him.

I don't blame him for needing security. Although, needing that at a police precinct seems a bit superfluous.

A couple of hours later, Dyson arrives in a three-car motorcade, all SUVs with tinted windows. The front SUV drops him off at the precinct entrance and he enters quickly, accompanied by a person in a suit. Except that this is no lawyer.

Willy Burrows is well known on the street and at the KCPD. His record may not be a mile long but it's getting there. Funny thing is, Willy could've been a lawyer if he wanted to. From what I know of his academics, he was destined to the Ivy League before the diversion to the wrong side of the law.

'This is my advisor. I take it he can be present during the interview?'

'We know Mr. Burrows here. His reputation precedes him. He can be present but I gotta warn you, any shenanigans and he will be out before he can arrange his necktie,' John cautions.

They are escorted to the witness room by a patrolman. Dyson and his lawyers are exchanging whispers when John and I enter, cans of diet coke in front of them, courtesy of the KCPD.

'This is being recorded. You are free to leave at any time,' I inform them.

'I am here to help any way I can,' Dyson declares, expansively.

'What do you know about Luc's murder?' John gets straight to the point.

'I know less than you. You guys have been all over this. You tell me.'

'You have taken over the leadership role, I understand.'

'Whoever said that? I am an adviser, is all. You know that.'

'We do know. And we know your record. Let me refresh your memory,' I answer back.

I push out his rap sheet toward him. Dyson and Willy give it a cursory glance. Dyson leans back and reaches in his right pocket. I'm not worried about a gun. He has been searched for weapons. Instead he fishes out a pack of cigarettes and takes one out.

'No smoking in here,' John interjects.

'Say what? I thought you wanted me to be comfortable.'

'It's not us. It's the CDC and Fauci and all that.'

Reluctantly, Dyson returns the cigarette back to his pocket.

'Did you take a good look?' I ask.

'Nothing new here,' Willy answers.

'Look. We have no information of any involvement on your part. What we don't want is bodies on the street. If that happens, we are going to come down hard. Put that word out there for anyone seeking payback.'

Dyson whispers in his Willy's ear and Willy whispers back his counsel.

'I'll make sure to keep the peace. But I will say this, it's not just me. The guys on the street, they need to survive.'

'We will be sending a message to the other side as well.'

Chapter XIX

Samuel

It's been a while since I last saw Tina. Truth be told, I've been too busy with my own personal stuff, little time for thinking about things. There are some issues on the financial front (when aren't there?) that I am dealing with.

I am walking home when I see a shadowy figure step out a few yards in front of me. I slow down, hesitating whether to proceed or to back off. I decide to do neither, just stand rooted to the spot.

The man has decided to approach me.

'You owe us money, dude,' he says, gruffly.

'Regarding what,' I ask.

'You know what. Don't act dumb. I need the money within three days, else someone gonna visit you. And it ain't gonna be pleasant.'

This is going back to my days of addiction. I thought I had paid off what I owed but that doesn't seem to be the case. Or, at least, I have someone here who disputes my understanding of it.

I am not going to just take in the threats this person is issuing, not without pushback. So, I start arguing about the details.

And it's in the midst of this arguing that Tina walks in. Actually, kind of, approaches slowly. I can see that she is surprised by the scene in front of her. The person arguing with me sees her as well and decides to withdraw.

'Remember what I told you,' he says, as a parting reminder, before retreating into the shadows from where he had emerged a few minutes earlier.

I have to admit that the encounter has left me a bit shaken. I did not think I would have to face this issue, not right now. But I turn my attention to Tina.

'What was that all about?' she asks. I can see that this has left her feeling rather nonplussed.

There was certainly menace in the words of the recently departed person. And come to think of it, I did not even ask him his name.

I am still catching my breath. After a few moments, I turn to her.

'Someone who came by to remind me of my past. I didn't think I would need to revisit that part of my life. But then, you never know.'

'We have a lot to talk about, then,' Tina replies.

I nod, more by instinct than with all my mental faculties. But I'm glad I did. We spend a long time talking. However, I must say that the earlier encounter has had it's effect. I am keenly aware of the consequences of not taking the threat seriously. And no matter what I feel about the demands, I have to address that and that too very quickly.

Once Tina has left, I try to gather my thoughts. And try to come up with a plan. A plan to either pay up or get the whole mess sorted out by appealing to a higher authority.

That is no easy plan. I don't think I will get a wink of sleep tonight.

Chapter XX

Anjie

Riley

I park my car into a side-street and make my way to a small alleyway. It's evening time, darkness is almost around the corner. I can barely make my way and I do not want to use my flashlight. Given Riley's worry about secrecy, I am in my civvies and the car is unmarked. About halfway down, sandwiched in between two dumpsters, I find Riley, dragging on a cigarette. I can see the glowing embers in the dark. He sees me approaching and throws the cigarette on the ground, squishing it with his boot.

Riley is a fascinating character for sure. A bad boy if ever there was one. The kind of person who, you would think, would be a great company to share a beer with. He is quick-witted and has a sharp mind. It's too bad he is not putting all of his gifts to better use than for petty crime and hedonistic living. I know, the usual story.

Here he greets me with a small wave of the hand and a Hi!

'Nice place for a meet,' I remark.

'Sorry. It's just that if I'm seen too frequently with you guys, I'm gonna be called a snitch. Nothing worse than that for business.'

'So, what you got for me?'

'Ok, I got something but not all that much. I spoke to this guy who sells these phones with SIMs. He remembers the numbers and he is pretty confident one of the numbers you provided is in that series. He says that he has no specific recollections of his clients. There were a couple of college kids who were looking for a bargain on a new model. One was a cute blonde. There was a tough-looking dude who looked like a bouncer at a nightclub. There was also one who he remembers but never saw his face. He had on one of them N95 masks and dark glasses. Anyway, he didn't ask too many questions.'

'What did this guy look like?'

'He looked like a muscular guy, six two or three. Dressed in jeans and light jacket. Beyond that, with a ball cap, dark glasses and mask, it was difficult to get much detail. He could id the voice. The guy haggled a bit and my guy had to reduce the price a bit to make the sale.'

'This guy, your guy, will he come in to the station and make an ID if it comes to that?' I ask.

'He said he will. But he needs a slight favor.'

Here it comes, I think. Nobody volunteers information just by the goodness of their hearts, especially when it could jeopardize you legally.

'So, spell it out,' I say, rather curtly.

'Thing is, this guy passed a bad check a couple of weeks ago. He did it unknowingly, though. He thought there were sufficient funds but turns out one of the creditors had taken out a lumpsum unexpectedly. If you can get the department to look the other way, he will come through.'

'I'll see what I can do,' I tell Riley.

First thing I'll need to do is to pull up this friend's rap-sheet and then discuss with Elsworth what kind of deal can be done. A murder investigation trumps everything else, save perhaps National Security.

This is a solid lead. Even an audio id can be critical. I watch Riley Walk away cautiously, looking around to make sure no one has observed our conversation.

I finish with my notes and follow Riley out a short while later. The alley has become really dark now. It makes me feel there is more than one rendezvous occurring here on any given night.

Alliance Citizens Bank, KC

The bank itself is on the corner of a street, just a couple of blocks removed from the busy downtown core. The entire front is glass, with a gold-plate coating that makes the glass resemble a mirror. It's not possible to see what's going on inside, not unless you press your eyes against the glass. This has given it a look of opulence and privacy and I'm sure the bank is doing very well. In the last few years, small and midsize banks have minted fortunes just by distributing government funds meant to keep businesses and citizens afloat during the pandemic. The parking lot, especially the spaces designated for bank officers, is replete with the latest models from Mercedes, Lexus and BMW.

I park my car near the front entrance and walk through the glass doors. Just inside the entrance is a sanitizer dispenser, now an ubiquitous presence across the commercial landscape. I walk over to the receptionist and flash my badge, informing her that I have an appointment with the manager. She looks at me and nods, then walks briskly down a corridor where the offices are situated. A few moments later, I am led down to the manager's office.

The manager seems like a pleasant person. She is dressed in a charcoal gray suit and skirt. She gets up and greets me affably.

'Detective Vilekar, I received your message and we would like to help as much as possible. I am just concerned about our clients' confidentiality,' she informs me, once we have settled down in our chairs.

I take a moment to answer. Getting a warrant will take time and even then, warrants are narrowly tailored to an affidavit.

'I appreciate that. This is a murder investigation. Our forensic accountant has identified three accounts in your bank that may have some transactions we need to follow up on. I must emphasize the 'may'. At this point none of your clients is in any legal jeopardy. If we find probable cause at a later date, we will draw up a warrant. You can be sure of that.'

The manager is lost in thought for a while. Then she looks up at me.

'What kind of detail do you need from us, at this stage, then?'

'At this stage, I only need to know the individuals identified with the business and the contact information. Needless to say, the bank will not be mentioned in our inquiries.'

'That sounds like a good plan. Let me see if I can get that information.'

She makes a couple of phone calls, giving the details of what I need. About twenty minutes later, one of the staff members walks in with a folder.

The manager looks inside and then hands the folder to me.

'I think you will find what you need in there.'

Two of the business marked by Esselstein are located in this bank. It's good bang for the buck. I take a look at the folder. Inside are the names of the business and the contact information for each account. The information for the contacts has been updated a year ago for one of the accounts and more than that for the other two. I will need to check the Dept of Revenue information on file for each of the contacts here. Just so I don't go banging on the wrong doors.

Another thing I notice missing is information as to when the accounts were opened. I mention this to the manager and within a few minutes, that piece of information is updated as well.

I spend the next few hours on the phone. I am able to get most of the information I need by the end of the day. But being that it is Friday, I will need to wait until Monday for some of the weekend vacationers to get back to me.

The photo and video shoot

My mom has her photo and video shoot planned for the weekend.

Every six months or so, my mother publishes a pamphlet for her patients, listing out healthy eating habits, exercises and a lifestyle that will help before, during and after pregnancy. The advice in the pamphlet follows the latest advances in nutrition and medicine from authoritative sources. The videos are posted on her website.

The whole session is generally done in the backyard. Some of the aquatic exercises are done in our pool. There is always a professional photographer and videographer. We know him quite well now, his being a regular for a few years.

I am up early this Saturday morning, even though my last evening was a late nighter. Nothing like looking up VICAP and law enforcement databases to spend time on a Friday evening.

Even so, my mother had asked me in advance to show up early. Early, meaning, in the morning. The shoot will be in the afternoon. During the first few years of the photo sessions, I was quite in the thick of things. Mom did the photography; dad and I were the set-up personnel. Ashwin was too young to participate. The editing and publishing were done in Dad's office. This was top-notch quality, though. He always had the latest editing and special-effects applications.

Now, the photographer/videographer does everything. He has his own staff. Toshihiro is very meticulous in his operation. Not even the smallest detail is overlooked.

I'm going a bit earlier. I feel like Ashwin has something on his mind. And I want to have a chat with him before the whole place gets busy with the folks arriving for the shoot.

When I arrive at the house, my mother is busy gathering material for the pamphlet. She is carrying a folder bulging with papers when she opens the door.

'Anju, I thought you would be arriving a bit later,' she says, in a bit of a surprise.

'Thought I might as well and grab some breakfast,' I reply.

I hadn't communicated to her that I was planning to chat with Ashwin. That would needlessly stress both her and my father.

'Oh, ok. I am a bit busy with collecting all the material. Will you help yourself?'

'Sure. You carry on. Where's Dad?'

'He's gone to his office. I think he misses his involvement.'

I nod in agreement. My mother goes back to her paperwork and I head to the kitchen. I realize that I am really hungry and quickly grab a sandwich and some coffee. Then I go upstairs and knock on the door of my brother's room. It's a bit ajar, not completely closed. Even so, I like to knock.

Ash is on his computer. He gives me a look that says What's up. I enter the room and perch myself on his bed. He wraps up quickly and then turns toward me.

'I wanted to see how you are doing,' I say to him.

'I'm ok,' he replies.

I really don't like to push him but I feel like I'm the one he would be most comfortable talking to.

'Last time I came by, I could see something was bothering you. I want to know what,' I say gently but like I mean it.

I guess that has an effect on him.

'My grades. I haven't told mom and dad yet,' he says.

I am a bit surprised. Ash usually has very good grades. And he's never been one to hide his grades from his parents. Or me for that matter.

'What's going on? If you're having a tough time with a subject or in general, you can let us know. We can get you some help.'

'I want to be a gamer. I don't think I want to continue studying.'

'Are you sure!?'

I am flabbergasted by this. Dropping out of school is something I never even considered. But then, Ash has his own life.

I am aware that professional gamers can make a good living. Many are celebrities on social media platforms, with seven figure incomes. But it is a competitive field as well. I am not sure how to respond.

I do know that making Ash do something against his will is not going to work. If he wants to continue with his education then that needs to be his choice.

'I think I am sure. I really don't feel like doing all these courses. I have no interest in all these subjects.'

'If you are just fed up with what you are studying, then maybe you can have a chat with your guidance counselor. They can point you to something that you enjoy while staying in school.'

Ash seems to be lost in thought.

'I'll see,' he finally says.

It's not just that I am worried about the gaming career that he might want to pursue. It's also the fact that his grades might deteriorate to a point where he may have trouble pursuing an academic career if he chooses to do so down the line. But another thought is nibbling at me: Are there other factors at play here? Is he being bullied at school perhaps, or more likely, on social media?

'Maybe you can have a chat with mom and dad. We can discuss together.'

'I'm going to. I know they are gonna be upset.'

'They may be surprised. But you know they want what's best for you. And maybe dad can help you as well. He knows the gaming industry quite well.'

Ash nods in tentative agreement.

I chat with him a little more. Obviously, I do not want to bring this up with my parents without Ash agreeing to it. But if I feel like the situation is getting worse, in regard to school work and his mental state, then I may need to insert myself, much as I would like to avoid that.

The lunch itself is a help-yourself deal. Mother is busy preparing for the day's activities. Ash is not really in the mood to eat anything and father is away at office.

So, I help myself to a sandwich and a coffee. And then I go up to my room and open my laptop and case files. Trying to match the connecting dots.

Right now, the lead I am following is the payment by Jacob to different business entities.

On the face of it they all look to be legit. So, what I'm looking for is longevity. The longer a company is in business, the more of a record they have and are likely to be scrutinized more as well. This is more a rule of thumb than a solid principle, but a good starting point all the same. After some analysis and my own intuition, I narrow it down to three entities. They are all in the KC metropolitan area, which makes my life easier.

Jordan is the first to join me. Rohan joins soon after. I work with them to arrange the exercise equipment and background. These will be used by some of mom's patients, in different stages of pregnancy. I thought this was a great idea when mom came up with it. And over the years, she has made it more fun and kept it equally educational.

Our part is limited now. Toshihiro has his own props that he has changed over the years. The exercise equipment is very much mom's, though. Once that is done, we deck out on the poolside chairs. It's a beautiful day, the sun is not too intense. And to be on the safe side, we have put on sunscreen. Jordan and Rohan know each other very well – and get along really well. So, the conversation is easy. After Jordan's searching questions about how things are going between Rohan and I, it's a great relief when Rohan diverts into his latest project. Though that doesn't last long.

There is some continuing tension between Rohan and I, from the incident in the parking lot. Rohan had wanted to be by my side when he saw that there was a possible threat. But I had firmly motioned him to stay away. It's not that Rohan cannot take care of himself. Rather, my concern was that any action he took could put him in legal jeopardy. It's not easy tell someone who cares about you to back off, even though you could use some help.

So now, on this occasion, Rohan has decided to vent his frustration.

'You shudda let me help you, then,' he says, remonstratively.

'Believe me. It was for your own good as well. I thought your presence could make matters worse.'

Jordan is watching a bit quizzically. She puts her arm around Rohan's shoulders.

'You know she's right. It's not like it would be if you were dating anyone else.'

I hope Rohan is satisfied by my explanation. That is the truth I gave him. In the back of my mind, at the time, were also headlines in the next day's newspapers.

'KC police detective arrests assault suspect.'

is a much better headline than

'KC police detective and boyfriend involved in scuffle in parking lot.'

Mom has been busy with her part but she now joins us. As an appreciation for our help, she has made thaalipeeth, a dish among my favorites. This, along with home-churned butter. Both Jordan and Rohan are foodies, with an appreciation of ethnic dishes. What can be better than this? And mom's tlc makes every dish she makes so much the sweeter. That's especially true when there are guests. I think she feels that guests would be quicker to pass judgment on her recipes from the old country. I don't think that's the case at all. In my opinion, it's more mom's constant quest for perfection, an ongoing battle. I do think, though, that having to prove herself, after starting from scratch, in a new country, has only served to make that quest, that drive, more all-consuming than it would otherwise have been.

Toshihiro arrives shortly after and then we have the photo and video shoot. What I like about this is that it takes my mind off all the problems that I face in my job. Those problems are still in the back of my mind, but at least not weighing as much. And seeing some of mom's patients, soon to enter into that new phase of motherhood in their lives, that gives a perspective on what is important. Not that catching criminals is any less important, but who we are fighting for in our society is important as well.

The whole session takes a few hours to wrap up and afterwards, myself and Rohan help clean up and put everything back in place. Jordan has already left. This would be also when I would normally spend some quiet time with Rohan, maybe grab a quick dinner. By now, I usually get the urge to get back to what is waiting for me on my office laptop.

But today I am not in the mood for chit-chat. Perhaps it was the conversation earlier regarding the parking lot incident. As well, Ash has been on my mind and I want to have a word with him to let him know he can count on me in whatever he decides.

So, Rohan departs and I walk back into the house. Dad has been home for a while but has kept a low profile. This is mom's day. And I think dad is happy to give her the space to do things her way. I exchange a few words with him and head to Ash's room. I see he is immersed in a book about commercial gaming. He is thinking about our conversation earlier and promises to call me soon. He is thinking of talking to his school counselor and maybe even a couple of his friends who are into gaming.

As I depart, I don't quite know how to frame the day. I feel like there is some unfinished business between me and Rohan. I don't know what I can do about it. At the same time, I am keeping secrets from my parents, even though the secret is not mine to tell. When I get home to by place, I am actually relieved when I see the one hundred plus emails in my inbox. I am glad to get back to the familiar, the certainty of knowing what to do.

Chapter XXI

Anjie

Shelley Downs

I am slowly working on my oat milk latte that I picked up a couple of minutes ago. This is the Starbucks store, having a busy time at rush hour as office-goers pick up their favorite before starting the grind. My eyes are on the woman who has just walked in to the store. I watch as she orders her drink and then looks around for an empty table, where she can quickly scan her phone.

Shelley Downs is a professional looking woman, mid-forties, dressed in a very nice jacket and skirt. She looks up at me as I approach, not sure for a second, before looking at me quizzically.

'Ms. Downs?' I inquire.

'Yes, do I know you?' Shelley asks, looking a bit flustered.

'Detective Vilekar, KCPD. I was wondering if you have a few minutes to spare.'

'Certainly. But how do you know me?'

'I hope you don't mind my approaching you this way. I saw your name outside your office when I visited the premises a few days ago. I had your address but I wanted to keep this informal and not ask you to come down to the station. I am looking for some help with Tina's case and I thought you might have some information that may be useful.'

I do not want to get into the details of the accidentally on purpose meeting that I spent a few hours on, including getting to know her morning routine.

'I don't know how, but I will do my best,' Shelley replies.

'I would like to request you keep this meeting confidential. I just don't want to raise any alarms unnecessarily.'

'Of course, you can count on me.'

'What is your function in the company? I assume you have an important post.'

'I am the chief of marketing. It is definitely an important job but you really earn your pay.'

'Has it been hard going?'

'It's always tough. We have a good client base but there is always competition lurking around the corner. And cheaper goods are constantly coming in, whether it's China or other countries. I think what sets us apart are the relationships we have built over the years. And our customers know that if anything goes wrong, we have their back. Mind you, we pay for this assurance with all the extra inventory we keep on hand. But that has kept us afloat even as some others have folded around us.'

'I noticed that your office is right next to Jacob's. I was wondering if Tina visited his office often or occasionally?'

'Jacob kept all kinds of hours, working into the night. The marketing is one thing but financing is another. If you have cash flow problems, that can really hit you. I think most of Jacob's time was spent on getting the numbers right. And then with our financiers. Tina came in once in a while. She had a stake in the business, she had inherited that on the death of her father. But she wasn't very active. All the reports used to go to her and she was one smart lady. As you probably know. You would have to be, to be in Gilchrist and then the apprenticeship as well at Burnham and Drexler.'

'Do you remember her last visit or some of her last visits?'

'Her last visit was a few days before her death. I'm not sure exactly when. I've been racking my brains about it. It was probably a week or so before. It was late at night. I was working on some of our sales and promotions.'

'Was it anything specific? Did they discuss anything? I'm sorry if the questions seem intrusive and I wouldn't ask if I didn't think it would help.'

'I understand. But to answer your question, I couldn't hear things too much. In fact, I often stepped out of the office for a while, just to not be eavesdropping. But I did hear Tina mentioning something about finances and Jacob was retorting somewhat angrily. There were some raised voices.'

'Looks like they were arguing, then?'

'Maybe so. They were brother and sister, after all,' Shelley grins.

I have to smile as well. Are there siblings who don't argue?

'Did you gather what any of the arguments were about?'

'I think I heard Tina say something to the effect "you know how to pick them." That was probably during her last visit, at least when I was present in my office. But I can't be certain that it was on the last visit.'

'Did they have arguments often?'

Shelley pauses for a moment while working on her frap.

'I wouldn't say so. I think it may have been a bit argumentative at times. But mostly, they were pretty friendly. I think they got along well.'

'Do you think Jacob was having an affair? Was there anything amiss that you noticed, personally or company-related?'

I don't think Shelley was anticipating such a personal question.

'I can't say for sure. If he was having an affair, he kept it discreet. It's not beyond the realm of possibility.

Regarding anything that concerns the business, I know that he worked with me and my team very closely on marketing and sales strategies and meetings. If he was involved in some financial shenanigans, I think it would be better to ask the finance guys and gals,' she answers, haltingly, putting some thought in each part of the answer.

This was to be expected as well. It was a long shot that Shelley may know anything about Jacob's personal life. But you won't ever know if you don't ask.

I thank Shelley for her time. She is in a hurry to leave as well, with the unplanned Q&A session. I look over my notes regarding the conversation we just had. Not much to go on. What were Tina and Jacob arguing about?

What exactly did "you know how to pick them" mean? Was it a bad investment? Or a girlfriend on the side? The number of possibilities is quite high.

Was it just a brother and sister thing? That is more of a possibility than anything else.

I decide to get down to the business of tracking down the payments. But first I got to get to the station for a follow-up.

A search warrant

Elsworth is in her office, on the phone in an animated conversation. Her door is closed. I station myself a few paces away and use the time to make a couple of phone calls. In a few minutes, the door opens and Elsworth walks out and looks in my direction.

'Vilekar, I thought that was you. Just what I expected Monday morning,' she says to me.

'Good morning, Lieutenant. I had to wait until Monday since you forced the time-off,' I reply, trying to match her tongue-in-cheek.

Elsworth is nothing if not a good sport. She laughs heartily.

'So, what can I do for you today?' she asks, seating herself in her chair and motioning me to take one as well.

I recount to her the conversation I had with Professor Sutton. Elsworth brings up the report I put in, to refresh her memory.

Then she looks at me.

'What are you looking for?'

'I would like to get any camera feeds from the hotel where the guests were staying. Also, lists of all the guests around that time. Their credit card information and records of any payments during their stay.'

I realize this is a somewhat problematic list, in terms of privacy but I may need it to narrow down the leads if something comes up. I don't want to be chasing warrants piecemeal.

'I'll see what I can do. The camera feeds should be available fairly quickly. The rest is a bit more complicated, as you are aware.'

I give my thanks and leave her room. I find John in his office. I give him a rundown of what's transpired. He nods his head. Something is on his mind.

'I was on a call with the DA this morning. The Jeremy Lloyd testimony is wrapped up. The closing arguments are happening today and should be wrapped up by tomorrow. The jury should have it by eod tomorrow.'

'Wow, finally. That's been going on for a while now.'

'Yeah. Five weeks. Thanks to the parade of witnesses and experts. It's a serious matter, of course. No denying that.'

'How's the DA feeling about the outcome?'

'It could swing either way. He's not as confident as he would like to be, I think. Kaminsky has sowed enough doubt about the whole affair. Whether it's reasonable enough for the jury is to be seen. If it results in a conviction, there's going to be some trouble on the streets. Elsworth has already laid out a plan of action to prevent any major disturbance. The judge will give us a heads-up a few hours before the jury comes in with the verdict. You and I will be there as well.'

I nod in agreement. It's been a lesson learnt over the years. Doesn't take long for things to go south and it's better to anticipate that than react to it.

'Give me a few minutes and I'll join you,' John says to me.

We have planned to visit the businesses on my short list. Depending on how things go, it may be a bust or could lead to something fruitful.

I decide to swing by Hansie's desk. He is engrossed in reading a graph.

'Interesting graph, anything I should know about?' I am trying to get his attention.

'Hey, Anjie. It's a mass spectrometer output. Trying to get some readings on the sample composition. And no, not your case,' he says looking back.

'Looks like we'll be getting the footage soon from the Tyler scene.'

'Ready for it. Hopefully, we'll get something. Although, honestly, I think it would've been more likely we would see something on the recent footage.'

'Would that we got some help once in a while,' I think aloud, *'de toute façon, tenez-moi au courant.'*

<<Bien sûr que si,>> he responds. Hansie is a bit of a language enthusiast and it's always fun to have a little repartee with him, in the language I picked up and grew to love during my year of study in Paris.

'By the way, have you been following the Ashes? Some serious bad blood in there. Ever since Wallace let fly a couple at the English batsmen,' he poses me the inevitable difficult question.

'Not really, but I'll try to get up to speed so we can talk about it when we view the footage.'

'Aye, aye, madam,' he signs to me, with a mock tilting of the cap. I grin and walk out.

John is already at my cubicle when I return. I get my stuff and we head down to the garage.

Knock and talk

The PR firm is first on my list. Anderson & Associates is located downtown in a modern office building. Their office occupies the entire fifth floor. The receptionist comes around from her desk once we have introduced ourselves.

'Mr. Anderson has asked me to show you right inside the conference room,' she says, walking down a corridor that has offices and meeting rooms on either side.

We take up our seats and moments later Anderson walks in, carrying a laptop. He introduces himself as Neil Anderson, the owner of the business.

He quickly set up the laptop and projects a presentation on the large screen at the head of the room. The presentation turns out to be a documentary of events that his firm has organized for their clients, including seminars, cookouts, press conferences, exhibitions and the like.

'We try to project our clients in the best possible light. Our job is to get their name out there and keep them connected with their communities,' he informs us.

'What specifically did you do for Jacob Adams's business?' Roman inquires.

Neil Anderson is ready for this question. He has another presentation that includes a couple of sales videos, several press releases, a Q&A session with Jacob and a documentary of the history of the business that shows its origin and development. Also included are charity events sponsored by the company and a message from Jacob.

'You are a rather new business. How did you manage to get this big an account so fast?' I ask.

'We are a new business but I am an old hand. I was with one of the well-known PR firms for a long time. We did not have this account but it is one of the bigger accounts around here. I ventured out on my own around two years ago and set up this firm. Jacob knows me from some of my previous work for his competitors. I was able to land his account since the no-compete clause did not cover this account,' Anderson explains patiently.

It all seems to be legit. As we are parting, Anderson hands us a glossy brochure about his firm.

'That looked like standard stuff,' Roman remarks, as we step outside.

I have to nod in agreement.

'I think we can cross him off our list,' I say as I literally take out my spiral notebook and cross of the name with my ballpoint.

Next on our stop is a firm that is listed as a positive influencer business. The business address turns out to be a mail box facility that has a receptionist who signs for any mail or deliveries. I identify myself and ask her about the business we are interested. She scans her computer and shortly comes up with an answer.

'Lena Hill, that's the person registered here.'

'She come in often to check her mail?'

'Every couple of days or so. She was in yesterday. So, she will likely be by tomorrow. We don't have a fixed schedule here. It's up to the clients.'

I ask for Lena's address. We will need to track her down. Just to check the name, I search the DMV database for Lena Hill. There are seven in the metropolitan area. I give the receptionist my card.

'Can you call me when she is next in?' This is an insurance policy. If we find Lena before then, no harm done.

She nods a yes and slips my card in a corner of her desk.

Lena's address is not far from where we are. We approach the place and I park the car on the street, which has a slew of No Parking signs. The meter maids have the car in the emergency vehicles list.

We walk up to the apartment listed and knock on the door. A couple of minutes later, it is opened by a middle-aged man, probably in his mid-forties.

I show him my badge. He seems a bit bewildered.

'We are looking for a Lena Hill,' I inform him.

'No idea who that is. I moved here two months ago.'

The landlord has no idea, either. Lena has not left a forwarding address.

'So much for a quick check,' I remark.

'I would like move on. We'll track her down when she checks her mail,' John suggests.

I concur with an ok and put the GPS on for the next name on our list.

If the offices of Anderson & Associates were glitzy, this place is a hole in the wall in a small strip mall a couple of miles out.

At the door, we are greeted by a young man, who gives his name as Sven. This is a business listed as a software development firm. Dad has a lot of competition. Sven lets us inside and we see six young developers, four men, two women, hunched over their workstations. Some are snacking while working on their keyboards. The room is not very large and brightly lit. There is an arcade-style gaming console in a corner of the room. I suppose this is to de-stress, a popular strategy.

'We are working on a plug-in for a leasing business, especially for seasonal-type equipment. It's well-suited suited for the farming sector. That way we can try to make sure that the equipment is idle as little as possible.'

'How did you get this assignment then?'

'We made a pitch to Jacob. We did about the same thing for a smaller company a few months back. But for this work, we need more staff and a slightly bigger space. I'm hoping that we could make an off-the-shelf product out of all this. That will make it easier to market. And maybe we will be able to move into better digs.'

As I watch, one of the female developers has decided she needs to de-stress, using the game console. Suddenly, bright lights start flashing with sounds of combat. The other workers are seemingly unbothered.

We leave Sven with his happy thoughts. There is no nefarious purpose here. Not unless it's really a small group of hackers, which seems unlikely. Jacob doesn't seem the type to hire an army of trolls or indulge in ransomware attacks.

'Does your dad have a game console for his developers?' asks Roman.

'I don't think so. They do have a volleyball court and a basketball court, though.'

'Hmm. Maybe I can get a job as a security executive at a place like that,' Roman responds with a laugh.

Now, we are left with the mail box receptionist to let us know when Lena comes in. If you think this all sounds like a lot of work with little to show for it, you are not alone. That's much of the way things go. Running down leads, most of which are dead-ends.

Chapter XXII

Anjie

Professor Nunes

We have Nunes at the station. Two students came forth during the inquiry to say that he had tried to solicit them as well, with a promise of better grades. Both claimed that he had graded them lower than they deserved so he could get what he wanted. One of the girls had flatly refused and threatened to report him, after which he corrected her grade. The other had seriously contemplated going along with him but did not do so, eventually. Which meant that so far, none of the students had fallen into his trap. But that's only as far as we know.

Nunes is seated in a small room at a metal table, on a metal chair. As we all know by now, there is a one-way mirror. Someone is always watching the proceedings in the room. There is also a live feed on a closed-circuit television.

Nunes does not have a lawyer. That can mean one of two things. Either he does not have anything to hide, or, he thinks he is smarter than the police and authorities.

I enter the room with John.

'Detective, I would appreciate it if you could let me know why I'm here. I'm a busy man and unless you have a compelling reason, I would like to leave, with your acquiescence.'

'I fully understand, professor. We wouldn't call you unless we felt we had a strong reason to,' John answers.

The professor seems miffed. I'm not sure whether it's bravado or just an act.

I lay out the documentation we have regarding his correspondence with his students, his attempts to solicit and documents that contain interviews with his prospective victims. The interviews and the correspondence documents have been redacted to conceal the names of the women who cooperated in the investigation.

'We have uncovered some correspondence between you and Tina that is, to put it mildly, quite disturbing,' I begin.

I hand him the printouts with the texts.

Nunes looks at that for a while. Then he pushes away the papers. He looks at us.

'There's no proof that any of this was from me. I categorically deny any involvement in this matter.'

'Not so fast. We have your IP address from your location at the coffee shop and we have traced other locations with the help of your ISP. So, you can deny all you want but we have you dead to rights on the correspondence and your attempts to proposition Tina. Not just that, we have had accounts from some of your other prospective victims. It looks like this was an ongoing activity on your part.'

Nunes has been listening intently. If he feels a certain dread, he is careful not to show it.

'Look, I'm not admitting anything. Any correspondence between myself and any individuals was strictly consensual. And I am sure that no laws were violated.'

He says this confidently. And being a law professor, he must believe that his opinions carry more weight than would otherwise be the case.

'We will see how that works out. At the moment I am interested in knowing if you had anything to do with Tina's murder. You can refuse to answer but if you give any false information, it could be construed as obstruction. You don't need me to tell you that,' I interject, trying to fluster his smug attitude.

Nunes mulls this for a while. Then he says,

'Hypothetically speaking, even if I did have that correspondence, there is no connection between that and the crime you are alluding to.'

'That may be. But if you look at it from my point of view, keeping all the stuff you were doing from coming out would be a pretty powerful motivation.'

He again thinks for a while.

'I was at my country cabin, about forty miles away the night Tina's body was found.'

'All alone?'

'Yes. I'm divorced for more than fifteen years. I spend a lot of time in my cabin. It helps me to think, once I'm away from the ceaseless cacophony of the city.'

'And you stayed there throughout the night?'

'Well, I went out for a stroll in the woods. And did some photography. I can send you the pictures. They should have a time stamp on them as well. Other than that, I was pretty much in the cabin the rest of the evening.'

I start to gather up the papers.

'What are you going to do about the stuff you say you have regarding my correspondence?' he asks.

'It's still under investigation. We will let you know if we need any further information from you,' I inform him tersely.

I am at my desk, when I receive a message from Elsworth, asking for a meeting. John texts me a few moments later:

Gather up all the info on the Adams case.

I wonder if perhaps she has heard from the college regarding Nunes.

Elsworth

John and I are seated in Elsworth's office. There is a knock on the door and Jordan walks in. Elsworth looks at us and starts.

'I hear Nunes has an alibi. Have we been able to check it out? It seems pretty thin to me, but nonetheless we need to rule it in or rule it out. Otherwise, it's possible we would find ourselves on a wild goose chase,' Elsworth holds forth.

'It's not easy to check. At the moment, we are trying to gather footage from any cameras that are enroute from his place to the cabin. But where that is, it's quite deep in the woods. No cameras there. We'll have to do some leg work with the neighbors. We've verified the photos he took and the timestamps but that doesn't cover the entire night or the time period we are interested in,' Roman answers.

'Ok, here's what I'm gonna do. I have arranged a meeting with the principal of the college tomorrow. I will discuss the evidence we have and I will be talking to the DA as well to see if there are any violations of the law. Since all the parties involved are adults, it might be difficult to get a criminal case. But the college is free to take action as per their policies. On another note, I'm assigning Det. Burns to work with you on this case and any other matters that may be connected. I know that Det. Vilekar and Det. Burns have a good personal relationship, so that is definitely a plus. Burns will prioritize this case. I've reassigned some of her cases so she can find the bandwidth when needed.'

I'm happy to hear that. John is a very reliable partner but we're chasing a lot of leads right now. Either of us could use Jordan on a two-person team and we don't need time-consuming approvals either.

Lena Hill

The mailbox receptionist has just called me. Lena has shown up and wants to access her mailbox. It's getting late in the evening. The mailbox facility is open until nine o'clock in the evening and it's just about closing time. I ask her to stall as much as she can. I make a quick call to Roman to let him know I am going to the facility and will try to keep an eye on Lena.

'Don't engage until I get there,' he cautions me.

With just lights, I reach the facility in less than ten minutes. I switch off the lights when I turn into the street and slide to the curb. I quickly text the receptionist to know the status. Her reply comes back:

She's leaving.

Moments later, a young woman exits on to the sidewalk. Her clothes are non-descript. I put her in her mid-twenties and height around five-seven. I confirm the description with the receptionist.

I am not interested in talking to her at this point. Roman's caution is noted. She gets into a small hatchback and pulls away from the curb. I watch as she passes me. After a couple of seconds, I pull away from the curb myself and start following her at a discreet distance. At this hour, the streets are deserted and it's much easier to spot a tail. Given that this young woman has no official address in the database, my objective is to found out her location and who she is associating with.

We leave the neighborhood and traverse through the streets. A while later, the residential neighborhoods give way to strip malls and shops, neon signs glowing in the night. I follow her on a street that has several restaurants and bars. A popular night life location. Lena pulls into a parking lot belonging to TJ's, a high-end strip joint. The parking lot seems to be half-full, it doubtless gets fuller as the night progresses. I pull over to the side of the road in one of the few empty spots left for paid parking. I whip out my phone to text the location to John. He texts me back quickly, indicating he will be there in a few minutes. He has been following my progress and is fairly close by this time.

The street is busy with night revelers. Some of the restaurants and bars are popular with millennials and Gen Zers. As research has shown, many of these generations are single (like me) and looking for reasons to spend their money, spend it on something worth remembering. Much of the popularity of some spots is attributable to TikTok and Instagram. An influencer can make or break a business in a day.

In my side-view mirror, I see John walking toward my car. I step out of my car and put on a sweatshirt. John is dressed casual as well.

'So, what's the plan?' John asks.

'Lena is in there. I would guess she is a dancer. I would like to have an idea about her work before we broach the subject of the payments.'

John nods.

'That's good. We still don't have a convincing alibi for Jacob. If Lena is his alibi, I would like to cross-check as much as possible.'

We walk into the club. Beyond a couple of metal doors, the scene changes from a quiet parking lot to loud music, strobe lights and a stage lit up in kaleidoscopic colors. The stage is unoccupied at the moment. John and I move to an empty table and settle down. I look around to take in the place. It's busy. A couple of waitresses are moving around quickly, zigzagging between the tables, bringing drinks to customers. Most of the customers are men, some single, some in groups. I do see a few women, in groups accompanied by men. These seem to be young professionals, likely come here straight from their offices.

A few minutes later, one of the waitresses shows up at our table. She looks at me quizzically.

'You here for an audition, hon?' she asks.

'Thinking about it. Just checking the place for now,' I reply.

'You should have no problem,' she says, smiling.

We both order non-alcoholic drinks and the waitress goes away to attend others tables.

'Well, that was a quick judgment,' I say with a laugh to John.

He nods, with a shrug of his soldiers. A new song starts and a dancer enters the stage. I realize after a moment that it's Lena. Her stage name has been announced as Lexi. Her makeup has changed now and she's hardly recognizable from the woman I saw not too long ago, picking up her mail.

Lena is an accomplished dancer and moves around the stage with grace and confidence. The fans sitting at the edge of the stage lean forward to stuff dollar bills in her stockings.

Toward the end of the song, the waitress arrives with our drinks. Mine is a Perrier with a twist.

'That's a good dancer,' I remark to the waitress.

'Lexi's good,' she agrees.

John pays for the drinks, with a generous tip.

'She a regular?' asks John.

'Lexi works Monday, Wednesday, Thursday nights. Thanks guys, enjoy yourselves,' she answers, flashing a bright smile.

I put forth my plan to John.

'If we want to test Jacob's alibi, I would rather interview Lena and Jennifer at the same time, separately. Less chance for Jacob to get a heads-up and try to fix things.'

'So what are you thinking?' John asks.

'Jennifer was in a meeting with her Japanese clients. If Jacob was not in his office, he was likely with Lena. That is, if the payment to her is what we think it is. If he wasn't, then we don't want him coaching Jennifer to provide him an alibi. Working on them simultaneously means less chance for them to sync their stories.'

'Ok, that sounds like a plan. I'll set up a time with Jennifer at the same time Lena is working here. I assume they are not all in communication with each other.'

'That's unlikely if Jacob is or was having an affair with her. Either way, we will be able to get to the bottom of it.'

We leave shortly afterwards. Lena has finished her dance and is now chatting with a group of people, accompanied by some of her fellow dancers. As I step outside after closing the door, I am struck by the comparative silence of the street. Maybe Lena is the key that unlocks the puzzle?

I pick up a cup of green tea on the way home. Nothing as soothing as that taste, no matter the situation. It's just around midnight when I enter my apartment. Mei is sitting at the dining table, her sketch in front of her, a set of pencils laid out. She is in the middle of doing a sketch and I take care not to disturb her.

She looks up from her sketch book.

'I got some extra soup if you are in the mood,' she offers, kindly.

Mei is generous to a fault and I almost feel guilty in refusing her offer. I settle into a chair opposite her, cup of tea in hand.

'Thanks,' I say, 'but I grabbed some dinner a while ago and a cup of tea on the way. I don't think it will go well with the soup. Is that a new design you are working on?'

She pushes her sketch book toward me.

'What do you think about it?' she asks.

I look at the sketch she has drawn. It looks familiar, very familiar but still there is something about it.

'Retro?' I answer, as a question.

Mei laughs.

'It's coming around. This is from the seventies. Making a comeback. The question is, how to make it look like you did not just lift it from the Vogue of that year?'

'Different shoes?'

'Louboutins,' she muses, 'I can see that. I'm trying to set off the material between the blouse and the skirt. Something that has a uniqueness about it. Maybe a pair of secretary sunglasses with a matching shade or all white.'

I finish my tea and retire to my room, Mei still very much absorbed in her project. It looks like an all-nighter for her. A warm shower later, I hit the bed, too tired to respond to the messages that have clogged up the screen all day.

Chapter XXIII

Anjie

The Jeremy Lloyd verdict

At seven am, I see an urgent message coming in. It's from dispatch. The jury has notified the judge that they have reached a verdict in the Jeremy Lloyd case. The judge will be convening the court in a couple of hours.

I am on the list of officers/detectives who are required to be present at the courthouse. We are expecting a large number of people to show up, both in support of Lloyd and against. There are those who think the case is one of entrapment and others who believe Lloyd belongs behind bars for the rest of his life.

I reach the courthouse and park my car in the designated parking area. John has arrived moments before me and he now lays out the plan for a small contingent of detectives. I am dressed in my uniform.

In a crowd control situation, one needs to be quickly identified as a police officer. It is quite jarring to see all the detectives in uniform. Not a sight that one sees often.

We take up our spots, marked out to give us the best possibility of success in preventing violence among the demonstrators who will be gathering. Even as the police are organizing, the crowd size has started to swell. A couple of participants have, very helpfully, put up large screen televisions. The verdict will be broadcast live and we will all be watching at the same time.

'How do you think its going to go down?' Jordan asks.

I shrug my shoulders.

'No idea. I think we had a strong case. But with juries, who knows.'

To be honest, I have a feeling that it may not be all that great a day for us. Kaminsky has likely planted enough doubt.

'The threshold for reasonable doubt has gotten lower. What with the public distrust,' quips Jordan.

She might as well have read my thoughts. And, for another dose of honesty, I have sometimes wished that verdicts would go against us, especially in cases where I felt that the state had not played entirely fair.

What about this case, though? I do not believe Kaminsky's version of the truth, or rather, his interpretation of the facts. He has turned the entire sequence of events into a well-orchestrated entrapment scheme. And it is only because of his – Kaminsky's – brilliance that the scheme has been exposed, with his incisive cross-examination and his analysis of the evidence, specifically the photograph with the microscopic red pixel.

Just after nine in the morning, the judge walks in and it takes another half an hour or so after that for the jury to be brought in. We can see the entirety of the proceedings on our phones or on the large screens put up outside.

Even before the jury pronounces its verdict, scuffles break out in the crowd. There is yelling back and forth. The minor scuffles are resolved quickly by the intervention of police officers, who are intermingling with the crowd.

Finally, the foreman of the jury stands up to deliver the verdict. It has to be unanimous. And it is:

Not Guilty

When I hear this, my heart sinks a little. At the same time, I feel a weight is lifted off my shoulders, given how much strain this trial has caused to the city and to the department. Now, it feels like we can breathe again. At least until the next similar case comes along, which, inevitably, it will.

There has been a momentary lull in the crowd, a silence where you can hear a pin drop. But then, suddenly, the jeering and heckling erupts anew, this time with a renewed vigor. It's as if the few moments of quiet were used for recharging. Now, placards are being brandished along with fisticuffs. Some of the ready folks have arrived with bear spray, which they are now using, with visible effect.

A little distance away, groups of people, openly carrying AR15-style assault rifles are standing, looking curiously at the proceedings. I am hoping no one will start shooting in such a hot melee. That would be absolutely catastrophic. Some of the officers ask the armed groups to move further away, which they do without much argument. A heavy police presence has kept the situation from deteriorating further. About a dozen people are quickly arrested. And around half a dozen are transported to hospitals with injuries. Jordan and I help load a couple of the injured into the waiting ambulances. It all seems to die down, albeit slowly. Some of the belligerent types remaining realize the futility of carrying on, with the added possibility of arrest and having to spend a night in county jail.

As things die down, Jeremy Lloyd and his attorneys walk down the steps of the courthouse to hold an impromptu press conference. More of a statement, really. And here, they rail against the high-handedness of the police, the unjust prosecutors and the injury to their client. They issue notice that Lloyd will be filing a lawsuit for damages against the city, with the tab coming in the millions.

Its well into the afternoon now. The crowd has dispersed after the press conference. After collecting all the equipment, we return to the precinct. Elsworth has called for a meeting to address the situation.

Elsworth is worried about the potential for continued violence. She wants us to be on alert for any planned disturbance and to use our CIs to gather intel about possible threats. And she wants to make sure that Lloyd is treated like any other citizen, without any animosity.

Nunes's cabin in the woods

It is well into the night when John and I approach Prof. Nunes's cabin. I cut the lights as I approach the cabin and park the SUV about a hundred yards away. There's only the moonlight coming through the trees to provide any kind of natural visibility. No lights in this part of the woods. John and I switch on our flashlights, in the firefly mode, to guide our steps. The property is pretty much unmarked. There is no fence around or anything to show the limits. Gingerly, we approach the cabin, a ramshackle structure, with a low-wattage bulb lighting up the front porch. There is no sign of anyone inside. None of the interior lights are on and I cannot hear anything moving. No car either. There is a bicycle that has been secured with a bike lock resting against the railings of the porch. It seems to be sufficiently old and worn-out that the lock feels redundant. We check the perimeter of the house and I take a peep in through the front windows and subsequently the back ones as well. No one inside.

'Not an evening for the cabin,' I say to John.

'Let's check out the surroundings,' John replies.

What we would like is some corroboration of Nunes's presence in the woods during the window of commission of the crime. The photographs he provided are not sufficient as an alibi. Nunes had stated that he pretty much stayed in his cabin for the night.

We get back in our SUV and decide to do a circular loop, with a half-mile radius around the cabin. If Nunes did venture outside, perhaps a neighbor could confirm his presence.

I drive away from the cabin until we are about half a mile away. Now the plan is to drive around in an approximate circle, so the radius is about the same along the way. This is easier said than done. The path I want to follow has no road, being so arbitrary. I need to dodge between trees and shrubbery. Thankfully it's an off-road vehicle. And there's also the fact that there's not likely to be any folks here at this hour. Even the hunters will come by much later.

I am doing my best to navigate the bouncy and improvised route. I estimate we are three-fourths of the way toward completing the circle (or close) when I spot a light some distance further away from Nunes's cabin. I would estimate that its around three hundred yards away from us. I look at John and he is thinking the same thing I am.

'Let's take a look,' he suggests.

I park the SUV some distance away. The thing about these places is that, often, visitors are not welcome. It's better to scout the terrain before making an appearance. We are both in civvies, badges tucked away. There are bright lights visible inside and there seems to be movement as well.

'What do you think?' John asks me.

'Something going on this time of night. I would say drug activity,' I answer.

'Best to just knock and see,' John suggests, as he steps forward.

The door is opened by a young man, dressed in a rather plain shirt and jeans. I notice that he is wearing an Omega wristwatch. Good taste and the money to support it. An older woman pops up behind him.

'What are you looking for?' the woman asks.

'One of our friends may have stopped by here?' John answers.

'Oh yeah, what kind of friend?' the young man asks.

'Can't say his name, but he is a professor.'

'You mean the guy that lives across there?'

'I won't contradict that.'

'Ok, that's fine. So, are you looking for the ket or the shrooms?'

The shack looks like a place that provides the psychedelic stuff to clients.

'Actually, we were looking for our friend and couldn't find him in his cabin. He was supposed to join us,' I answer.

'He isn't here. If you want to get your stuff, you'll have to put up a deposit. Then we can talk,' the woman informs us brusquely.

'I think we will come back later with our friend,' John says.

'So that's a shroom den. And it looks like Nunes is a customer,' I remark.

'They are not the type to keep visitor logs. We will need to corroborate his alibi, or break it, some other way.'

I look around the place. Nunes's cabin is some distance away. There is no road connecting the shroom place and the cabin.

'I wonder if there are any cameras around here,' I say to John.

He looks at me and nods.

'We can take a look around. There are some hunt clubs that operate in this neighborhood, especially for pig hunts. They may have some installed to track movement.'

We put our flashlights on bright and start looking up the trees, starting with those on the path between the two shacks. It's a large area to cover. After an hour and a half, I spot one on a tree, below one of the low branches. It's still to high to grab, even using the SUV as a makeshift ladder.

I take some pictures with my phone, trying to zoom in as much as possible to get a clear shot of the device. Hansie may be able to glean more information using filters and AI. I am hoping they store the records long enough for us to see the footage of the night in question.

Sarah Donalds

The descent into Atlanta includes a view I always enjoy – the skyline of the city, the biggest of the South. Sarah Donalds was traced as living there in the downtown area. She has been using the alias Tracy Davis. This looks like an alias made out of whole cloth. There is no evidence of Sarah having used that name before. There are still some questions about how she is sustaining herself, but the accounts that were in Sarah's name in KC were cleaned out. The suspicion is that Sarah may have been living off the cash from those accounts and has, maybe, access to other funds that we are not aware of.

After landing, I take an Uber to the local precinct, from where the information regarding Sarah was relayed to KCPD. The traffic in downtown Atlanta is always a gauntlet. For some time now, the city has transformed from a southern city to a metropolis, having more in common with the large metropolises like NYC and Chicago than with the south. The population is as diverse as anywhere on the face of this earth. And the downtown area has grocery stores and restaurants that can satisfy the longings of home cuisine for any inhabitant or visitor.

With the reciprocity laws, I can legally carry my service weapon to Georgia. That's always helpful, rather than needing an escort. In this case, however, one of the detectives will be accompanying me for the interview with Sarah.

I identify myself to the desk and am shown to a conference room. Pretty soon after, a man and a woman enter the room. I know both of them from the zoom call I had yesterday.

'Hello, Detective Vilekar. I'm Lt. McNabb, this is Detective Lawson. We met on the call yesterday,' the woman introduces herself and her colleague.

After a quick round of handshakes. McNabb continues.

'Now this lady, Tracy Davis, or Sarah Donalds, she has been living in Georgia for some time, according to the information we have on her.'

'She is working with a grocery store chain, where she is the Assistant Manager. She has an account at a local bank. We haven't been able to determine if she has other sources of income. But Tracy does not seem to be living outside her means. If we want to get more detailed information, we're going to need a warrant and, at the moment, we don't have probable cause for getting that signed off,' Lawson gives a rundown. His voice has a hint of a southern drawl, giving him an air of not being in too much of a hurry.

I nod in agreement.

'We don't think Tracy is involved in the homicide. And we're not really interested in her financial activities. For now, I need to get her story. She may or may not contribute to the case moving forward. But we won't know until we talk to her,' I inform my Atlanta colleagues.

'So, from what I understand, you are just looking for an interview, a voluntary one. Tracy has not broken any laws in Georgia, from what I know. Detective Lawson will accompany you during your stay. Hope it's a pleasant one.'

McNabb gives me a nod and walks out of the room. Lawson is checking his phone and looks up after a short while.

'Tracy is in her apartment right now. We can drive over and get this done,' he suggests.

I concur. I have brought along a folder containing some details that may help during the interview.

We park on the street, just opposite the building. Construction work is going on all around and workers in hard hats are toiling in the Georgia sun. Lawson and I walk up to the entrance. It's locked and requires a buzzer. Lawson punches in the code for the manager and identifies us. The door opens quickly.

We decide to take the stairs to the fourth floor. Nothing is as unproductive as being stuck in an elevator. I ring the doorbell and it's opened shortly after. The woman who opens it reminds me of Tina Adams. Approximately the same age, close to the same build. She is surprised to see us. I step forward and quickly identify myself.

'Tracy Davis?' I inquire.

'Yes,' Sarah replies, nodding in the affirmative.

'I am Detective Vilekar, Kansas City PD and this is Detective Lawson, Atlanta PD.'

Hearing 'Kansas City' seems to have had an effect on Sarah. She is not quite so sure of herself anymore. She, however, gathers herself after a moment.

'How can I help you?'

'I am here pursuing a homicide investigation in Kansas City. Detective Lawson is my local liaison. May we come in?'

Reluctantly, Sarah moves aside to let us in. It's a nice apartment with decent furniture. We take our seats.

'Look, Tracy, I want to let you know that we are not investigating you of any wrongdoing. I think you can help us bring the killer of Tina Adams to justice. Detective Vilekar has come in from Kansas City to see if you can provide any information that may help resolve the case. I think it's in your best interest to cooperate. This is a voluntary interview. Are you ok to proceed?' Lawson informs Sarah, asking for consent.

Sarah nods slowly, indicating the affirmative.

'I need you to say Yes or No,' Lawson prods gently.

'Yes.'

I take out my folder with the material that we have gathered over in Kansas City. In particular, Sarah's presence in the matter, nebulous as it is.

'Hi Tracy. I want to confirm that you are Sarah Donalds, living in Kansas City, until approximately the death of Tina Adams. Is that correct?' I start out for the record.

Sarah is unsure of her answer. After a long pause, she lets out her breath.

'That is correct. I was living in Kansas City and using the name Sarah Donalds.'

'And that's the name you were using when enrolled in Gilchrist School of Law in Kansas City?'

'That's right.'

'And you would prefer to be called Sarah or Tracy? It does not matter to us.'

'I would like to be called Tracy.'

'Tracy, I would like to know if you had any contact with Tina Adams, either in-person or by any other means?'

'I met her once when I went to see a play in the theater. I used to take part myself. Tina was a very good actor. Brilliant. She brought her part to life so vividly. Underplaying but stamping her authority on it.'

'You talked to her on that occasion?'

'We chatted for a while after the performance. I remarked on her talent and she thanked me for the compliment.'

'Anything else?'

'We talked about our experience in the field of law. I had been through some tough times financially and we talked about how the pay is not great for starting out, especially since most students have a load of debt that they are constantly under pressure to pay off. I also had a couple of hustlers try to get some inside information of cases within the law firm I was working in. I mentioned that to her as well.'

'How did she react?'

'I think she was a bit surprised but not completely. After all, skullduggery in litigation is hardly unknown.'

'As regards the time when you were contacted for the inside information, can you describe that episode?'

'Someone, a woman I think it was, contacted me over the phone. She described herself as a journalist and a reporter on court matters. She wanted information on something that our firm was dealing with. There was a particular court case that our firm was working on. A multi-million-dollar litigation that was eventually settled in favor of our client. This person wanted to know the progress and what our brief was going to be like. She said there would be good money in it if it turned out to be a scoop. I didn't do it, of course. I was in a bit of a financial mess but I certainly didn't want to get caught up in anything like this. It didn't sound very ethical.'

'And that was that?'

'There were a couple of calls from this lady. But then, I replied that I was not interested and that stopped.'

'Which was your law firm, where you were employed at?'

'I was at Turweiler & Associates.'

'Did you mention this to your law firm?'

'Yes. I did. They asked me to cut off any contact with anyone regarding the matter. I did not hear anything after a firm no a couple of times.'

'Did you subsequently speak with this person again?'

'I did. I called them some time ago. I was having some difficulty with my finances again. I wanted to see if I could get some help from this person. I called but no one answered. After a few days I heard back. It sounded like the same person who had called in the first instance. She told me that she needed some information about a litigation going on. If I could get the right information, I could get upto twenty thousand dollars. I wasn't sure about this. I offered to analyze legal cases since the woman had stated she was a legal reporter. But I was not willing to put myself in legal jeopardy. I got the feeling that she wanted me to get the information from a legal firm maybe by using subterfuge, you know, Wall Street style. She didn't want any help from me in terms of legal analysis.'

'Did she mention which particular litigation she was referring to?'

'She said it was a major litigation regarding a takeover. She mentioned Drexler & Burnham. Asked if I know anyone there.'

'Did you answer that question?'

'I said I didn't know anyone. I certainly wasn't going to involve anyone I knew. I already had a feeling that it could lead to trouble down the line.'

'Did it go any further?'

'When I told her I couldn't do anything that could put me in legal jeopardy, she didn't pursue.'

'Why did you decide to leave town and change your name?'

'When Tina was murdered, I then read about the merger she was involved, even though the news reports didn't specifically mention her name and the merger together. But I knew that the firm she was working for was involved in the merger negotiations. The more I thought about it the more I panicked. I felt like I was a loose end and they could just as easily decide to come after me. As for the name change, I haven't really changed my name. On my birth certificate, I have both the names Tracy and Davis from my maternal and paternal side. It took a bit of effort but I have been legally able to exist as Tracy Davis. I hope you are not going to make my life more difficult. I am actually hoping to come back to Kansas City at some point in the near future. I feel like I'm the fugitive, living in fear. I'd rather face the danger there and live my life. If you guys manage to catch the killer or killers, that would really be a load off my mind.'

I am taking down all the notes I deem important and the interview is being recorded as well. I have to say that I feel a great deal of empathy for Sarah. I do have one more question, though.

'You said you thought it was a woman. Are you not sure? Was the voice ambiguous in any way?'

'I am fairly certain it was a woman. It could be a man with a feminine voice or an AI-produced voice, although I don't think I could distinguish that from a normal voice. I've heard that they can proceed voices that even parents and friends cannot discern as artificial.'

I mull that over. Then I close my folder and look across at Lawson. He is the lead here and he may have some questions of his own. He indicates he does not.

'Thank you, Tracy. I hope you come back to Kansas City. Contact me if you feel like you need any help, even a person to just talk to. I will do my best to make sure you are safe and comfortable.'

Lawson gives her a slight nod as we leave the apartment.

'Hanky panky in the legal, who woulda thunk it?' he asks sarcastically.

'Big bucks, big stakes. I still don't know that's the reason Tina was murdered. But it's the seamier side of the business, for sure.'

I still have some time for my flight. I had kept an hour as a buffer just in case Sarah was not available very quickly. I always assume my check-in will be quick, with the special processing for law enforcement. I whip out my phone and send Roman a brief outline of the interview. He sends me a thumbs up emoji in return.

Lawson is looking at me.

'Is there anything you want to do in Atlanta? With the time you got?' he asks.

I can think of a place. It is one of my favorite dessert spots whenever I visit the city.

'I think we can stop by Butter & Cream if that's ok by you.'

Lawson laughs out.

'You know your Atlanta. I can think of nothing better.'

A short time later we are at Butter & Cream and I am going through the list of flavors. I settle on the Ethiopian Harrar Coffee. One of those delicious flavors that I rarely see in other places. The coffee has a taste of its own, grown in the high altitude of the Oromia region of Ethiopia.

Lawson has chosen the old favorite – Butterscotch. Can't go wrong with that, either.

We settle on a table. I don't want to take this outside for it to melt in the Atlanta heat.

'What do you make of her?' Lawson asks me.

'I think she is or was genuinely scared. It hit too close to home. I'm not sure that it had to do with her legal work. But it's an avenue that I need to chase down.'

I finish the scoop, taking my time to enjoy the deep flavor.

'I gotta ask. Are you single or seeing someone?' Lawson asks.

I give him a sincere smile.

'Got a steady boyfriend. And I gotta say, it's going pretty well so far. Better than some of my previous relationships.'

'I thought as much. But I'd be kicking myself if I didn't ask,' Lawson says with a smile.

The airport is crowded, as usual. My security is very quick but it doesn't help that the flight is delayed due to some weather on the eastern seaboard. An hour and a half of delay. I take the time to catch up on my Taylor Swift and go over the interview notes. The obvious question is whether Sarah was involved in any way in the same merger that Tina was working on. And who was the woman (assuming it was a woman) that was on the other end of the line? If indeed the person was not a genuine reporter but a manipulator, the motive is clear. It's the money.

There is a light drizzle at the airport when we land. Rohan is there, waiting patiently. He has tracked the flight on Flightradar. He hands me a cup of green tea. On the way home, I pick up a salad and sandwich. The taste of the Ethiopian Harrar Coffee lasted a long time.

Cameras in the forest

For a change, Hansie has strolled over to my desk.

'Need to get out more,' he says, laconically.

I am not sure if he means the great outdoors or just out of his comfortable office.

'Did you get anywhere with that?' I ask, referring to the camera we spotted near Nunes's cabin.

'I was trying to find the hunt clubs that operate in that part of the woods. There are three big-sized clubs. Two of them share the footage. The third is a rather exclusive club that operates its own equipment. I've sent the camera specs to the clubs and asked for the footage for the last six months. It won't hurt to have additional footage in case we draw a blank with that.'

'Did they say when they can get that?'

'In a day or so. They usually store the footage in the cloud and members can view it. They mostly track feral pigs but also predators. In addition, they want to make sure that none of the hunters are there illegally. The clubs pay good sums to the property owners to hunt on their land.'

'Well, I've referred the shroom operation to the vice division. Not that I want to interrupt their pleasure trips or treatments but I'm not sure about the expertise of those administering them.'

'A quiet place for getting high. Maybe that's what the clientele wants instead of a clinical setting and a chair in a doctor's office,' Hansie muses.

'We'll see how this professor's alibi checks out. He's already in a heap of trouble though,' I shake my head.

I get another surprise when Elsworth pops her head in my office. I am in the middle of filling out my field report.

'Detective Vilekar, you have a few minutes to spare?'

I nod my head. Roman is out in the field.

'Give me a second here,' I answer, trying to save my work and make a couple of notes.

'Walk with me,' Elsworth says.

'Look, detective, we have a bit of a sh*tshow here, as regards Nunes. I've postponed my meeting with the college until we get some solid info regarding his involvement in the Adams murder. Either he's in or he's out. I want you to follow up with the hunt clubs and confirm whether he is a suspect or not. What I don't want to do is give them this info and hit them two days later with a newsflash that he's also a suspect in a murder of his student.'

I nod. Elsworth is right, as usual.

'But I also don't want Nunes running around unrestrained. I've got a unit on him, doing hourly checks. And I want to work with Hansie to keep monitoring his online activity so we can pre-empt anything nefarious, if need be,' Elsworth continues.

'Now, as regards our witness in Atlanta. That's an angle that is plausible. What do you think?'

'It's possible. There's a lot of money involved. I wouldn't rule it out. Only, there's no direct link. At least not yet.'

'How are you playing this simultaneous interview with Jennifer and Lena?'

'I am going to interview Jennifer at her residence, I guess her home office. That's about the same time, but maybe not exactly, when John will talk to Lena after she comes in for work. We don't want to forewarn of a police interview by talking to the manager.'

'And what if she doesn't come in?'

'We'll call the club to make sure. John can always pretend that he is a regular who comes in to see her.'

By this time, we are at our small cafeteria, which comprises mainly a coffee machine and a couple of vending machines. Elsworth makes a cup of coffee and offers it to me. I can use one. Then she makes one for herself.

'I just wanted to mention to you that this is a high-profile case. If we crack this, your career is likely to take a turn for the better, pretty fast. I am taking note of your commitment and your perseverance and so are others in the department. I'm old school myself and I think there is no substitute to shoe leather work.'

This is heartening to note. Always good to hear that you are doing something right. Right now, though, we have yet to go some way to find justice for Tina.

Jennifer and Lena

It's approaching eight pm in the evening when I park my car in front of Jacob and Jennifer's residence. We have a time when Jacob is out of town and Jennifer is working late, preparing for a meeting with clients on the other side of the world, in Asia.

I had to give a rather convoluted story about the time for the meeting. Even so, John and I thought it was better to do it this way rather than put a tail on Lena and then try to catch a time when both the ladies are simultaneously available and cooperative.

Lena's shift at the club starts at seven in the evening. So John has planned to arrive near to eight pm. We have cross-checked to make sure we are conducting our interviews at approximately the same time.

I find the house quiet but well-lit when I ring the doorbell. Jennifer opens the door. She is in office clothing, the kind you need for a formal meeting.

'Do you mind if we talk in my office? I have a meeting coming up soon and I need to send some emails before that.'

I signal my ok and we go through the foyer. Jennifer's office is a relatively small room but well-furnished. On the table is a laptop with a monitor on either side. They say that the more the number of screens, the higher the productivity, although the limit is three screens. After that, I guess, remembering what you were doing and where negates some of the gains.

Jennifer takes a seat. Her chair is a low-back type as opposed to the high-backed ones that have a neck support. There is a tag still visible.

'New chair,' I remark.

'Yes, got it a couple of months ago. I find that I like to lean back while working and the high-back chairs are not great for that,' she says with a laugh.

I can relate to that. I find leaning back helps me think at times by taking my eyes off the desk.

Jennifer is working on her emails. I want to avoid raising alarms during this interview, although I recognize that's not completely avoidable.

The backdrop behind Jennifer is already familiar to me. I saw it before on the video of the meeting that Jennifer sent across. Her alibi. A pretty and colorful map of the world that was made by a Japanese artist.

'Thanks for meeting me at this time and I apologize for the late hour.'

'That's not a problem. I usually have meetings that go well into the night.'

'We were trying to corroborate some of the testimony as part of our investigation. You said earlier that you were in a meeting from ten pm to approximately ten-thirty pm, is that correct?'

'Yes, that is correct. As I recall, the meeting finished a couple of minutes before ten-thirty.'

'And during this time, did you receive a call from your husband or anyone else?'

'No, I did not.'

'Did your husband return to the house while you were working?'

'No. I didn't see him until early in the morning.'

'Do you remember what time you went to bed?'

'I remember working for around two hours after the meeting. That's approximate.'

'Jacob came back after you were in bed, then?'

'Yes. Now, what is this about? Is Jacob a suspect? Am I a suspect? I thought we had answered all your questions.'

'We just need to corroborate the testimonies we have before we can rule things out. I really appreciate your time and your accommodation regarding the hour.'

'Happy to cooperate. Good night.'

I get the feeling that Jennifer wasn't too pleased with the way the interview went. But now, I know that Jacob wasn't home and he wasn't in his office. So, it depends on what Lena has said to John and Jordan.

I text John as I leave the house to let him know I'm done with the interview. He calls me back soon after. I'm driving to my apartment, there is no need to go back to the station at this hour. I can have a zoom call with John and Jordan later, if necessary.

'Lena's testimony is that he was with her that night. She remembers that because she heard about Tina the next day. Kind of hard to forget, as well,' John gives me an update. He is driving alone. We are heading back home, done for the night.

I relay to him what I discussed with Jennifer. John is silent for a moment.

'Jennifer didn't note the time Jacob came back?' John wants to know.

'No, she did not. She said it was early the next morning, before the sun had risen.'

'Well, it's not airtight, so we'll have to keep him on the list. Anyway, let's regroup in the morning to see where things stand. I feel like we are getting to the point where the rubber is hitting the road for the first time.'

I hang up and start thinking about my hot shower before flopping down on my bed. But, again, the best laid plans….

I am less than a mile away from home when I get a call from dispatch:

There is a young male named Samuel Bishop who is at the precinct regarding the Tina Adams case.

Samuel

I turn my car around, heading back to the precinct. John and Jordan are on their way as well. Since we are now working together, it would be useful to hear this witness together, in case he turns out to be useful.

I reach the station the earliest. Bishop has been placed in a witness room, a spartan environment if ever there was one. But, I see that he has been provided a coffee and a sandwich that he is nibbling at as I arrive. I do not enter the room. I am observing from behind the one-way mirror. The officer who has been watching so far greets me with a nod.

'Seemed like he was hungry.'

'Let him finish. Roman and Burns are on the way as well. Maybe this is the guy that blows it wide open. Anybody talk to him so far?'

'Nothing beyond getting his name and contact info. Once he said he has relevant info, we thought it's better to get your team in here.'

'Good thinking. I'll take it from here.'

I'm watching Bishop as he works on his sandwich and coffee. He seems a bit nervous. Totally understandable. There are few people who are at ease at police stations. Lawyers come to mind as one of those types.

It's around fifteen minutes before John and Jordan reach, back from their respective routes home. We are all in the preview room.

'How are we going to tackle this?' I ask. Roman is the senior detective and he will direct the questioning. By now, Elsworth has been informed as well.

'You and I go in. Burns stays outside. He is a volunteer witness. Let's see what he has to offer.'

That's the plan of action. We get the case file together and a short while after, John and I enter the witness room, with Samuel Bishop sitting opposite.

Samuel (I'll use the first name) has finished his sandwich and is slowly working on his coffee.

'I am Detective Vilekar and this is Detective Roman. You have some information for us,' I introduce us to Samuel.

Samuel looks at us in turn and gives a polite smile.

Over the next two hours, Samuel gives us his version of events, much of it is a side that we have not encountered in our investigation.

The question to pose is obvious, but from Samuel's story, the answer will be simple.

'Why are you coming forward now, after all this time?' I ask him.

Samuel looks at me, then shakes his head.

'I couldn't come sooner. I was in hiding after I heard about Tina. I was sure that Garz would be looking for me. So, I was hiding off-grid. I couldn't dare to use a cell phone either. Number one, I knew I needed to come in so you could believe me. But more than that, I was hoping you guys would arrest Garz and then it wouldn't be on me to finger him. But when I saw that that was not happening, I decided to do something. I couldn't stay in hiding forever. I had to come out.'

'Did you know Garz before your interaction with him on that day when he came by to threaten you?'

'No, that was the first I met him.'

'And did you meet him subsequently?'

'No, I never met him, but I was trying to get some info on him. I didn't get very far, so I decided to stay in hiding until now.'

'Did you get to know his identity other than Garz? That sounds like a street name.'

'I couldn't find that out. I suppose Garz is his street name, but he could be going by another name on the street. That was the name he gave me, for what it's worth.'

Samuel looks a bit frazzled after the long session. But there are a lot of questions. If this person, Garz, is behind the murder, then, needless to say, apprehending him is a priority. However, there is no probable cause at the moment to effect an arrest, much less bring the case to a prosecution.

First things first, though. Who is Garz? This is the first I have heard of him. And John and Jordan seem to be in the same boat. It would be a fake name that he just used while trying to intimidate Samuel. But, we need to get to the bottom of that.

'Let's get Stevens in on this. Vice may have a clue on someone going around using that moniker,' John suggests.

'What about this guy? If what he says is true, he could be in danger. Especially if they find out he snitched,' Jordan inquires.

'If he doesn't want to be in protective custody, there's not much we can do. Not at this stage.'

'How about a material witness warrant?' I put forward a way out.

'We need a bit more for that. Let's dig up something on Garz. In the meantime, I'll ask Bishop to lie low and give us an address.'

Samuel is not willing to get a protective detail.

'I think I'll be a sitting duck if they spot me. And if they see a cop squad around, the word will spread pretty quickly.'

Samuel looks scared. And I think it's a justified fear.

He gives us an address where he can be reached. As he walks out of the door into the dark of the night, I cannot help but wonder if we will see him again.

'I'll ask an unmarked to do a drive by at his address every hour, nothing obvious,' I chime in.

John nods his head in agreement.

'Let's play it loose until we have something more solid. We don't want him going into hiding again,' he adds.

Finally, I'm headed home. But what I expected to be a night of restful sleep has now been turned over. I don't think I'll be able to even nod off.

Going back to my apartment, I find the roads quiet. It's almost three in the morning. There is the occasional delivery truck and the Uber. The Ubers are far more common than the regular taxicabs. And there are some shift workers as well, either going to or finishing their odd-hour shifts.

My apartment is dark. Mei has probably gone to bed long ago. I do need and take that hot shower quickly and then open my laptop.

The search for 'Garz' yields no results. Just a bunch of similar sounding words, no connection to any real person. I search for 'Samuel Bishop,' the name of the witness. Here, the results are plentiful. No surprise. But there is no one resembling the witness. So much for Google. I look into all the databases, including VICAP – the Violent Criminal Apprehension Program of the

FBI. No hits either. It looks like Samuel Bishop is a quiet person indeed, who has kept pretty much to himself.

By the time I have finished, I realize that the sun will be up in less than two hours.

Chapter XXIV

Anjie

The Hunt Club Cameras

Hansie is waiting for me when I enter his cabin.

'I found some footage that might be useful,' he declares when he sees me.

'Our prof has an alibi?' I ask.

'Kinda. You will see.'

He scrolls through some files on his computers and selects one to play.

'The good thing about the cameras is the resolution. They need it to identify the animals, including whether each can be identified individually.'

He is playing the video. On the screen, there is not much movement beyond the tree branches swaying in the wind.

'I've started it a few minutes before the prof comes on the screen. So you get the lay of the land.'

A pig runs into the frame and looks around for a moment before darting out of the frame. Not long after that, Nunes is seen entering the frame. If I remember my geography correctly, with the positioning of the camera, he is walking from his cabin toward the mushroom shack.

'Now, this is about an hour before the earliest time the murder could have happened. And about an two hours before the latest time that the ME has specified.'

'Do you have him coming back to his cabin?'

'Not on this camera. But here is the footage from another three hours later.'

The footage shows Nunes walking rather languidly back to his cabin. His face and features are recognizable even though the camera is positioned a distance away.

'This is the path back?' I ask Hansie.

Hansie shows me the position of the camera that has captured the footage. Looking at the placement and the direction, it's clear that Nunes is walking back to his cabin.

So there's his alibi. Nunes was not physically present at the scene of the crime.

One thing I am sure of. Even though he may have no involvement in the homicide, the investigation has saved some future victims from his predations.

Garz

Elsworth's office is pretty much full. There's more officers in there than I can remember seeing in a long time. I see Ray Stevens from Vice and a couple of other officers, one of whom, I know for a fact, is working undercover on a narcotics detail.

John and Jordan are seated in front and there is an empty seat next to Jordan where Elsworth signals me to take a seat.

Jordan has been doing research on Samuel alongside me and briefs the group on our findings.

'Samuel Bishop is not in any of the databases we looked, that includes state, local and FBI. We haven't checked Interpol so far. We have sent out a query to the DC office but it will take them a few days to get back. That is, however, more hope than substance. From what Samuel has told us, he has been living in Missouri and Indiana most of his adult life.. Some travel to Mexico. We are checking those leads as well. More importantly, we have nothing to connect him to the murder of Tina. He claims he was at his restaurant working late, around the time of commission.'

Elsworth is listening intently, along with the rest of us.

'How credible is his story? I think we have to take it at face value and get to the bottom of it. Especially since we don't have a suspect to effect an arrest on. Even if we did, we have to run this down. I don't like the idea of loose ends being left untied.'

Elsworth looks at Ray.

'Any idea who this fellow Garz could be?'

'I've been trying to comb my sources. No one with this street name comes to mind. I'm inclined to think it's a low level guy or someone who just hasn't ventured out in the street much. Likely an up and coming enforcer. We may run across him in due time but nothing yet. I am leaning hard, so if it's someone legit, I could hope to get some info soon.'

'The team is working our sources as well. If this guy was involved in the homicide, he could be laying low. May have even left the state for a while until things cool down.'

'Ok, let's put some manpower behind this. Your team will coordinate with Vice to tap as many sources as possible. If we have to get some help with external jurisdictions, let me know.'

She turns to me.

'Detective Vilekar, where are we with the professor?'

I give her a summary of the findings with Hansie and my own research.

'Ok, that looks like a solid alibi. At least we are able to cross his name off this list. His other activities are another matter, though. I will be speaking with the State's attorney about it soon enough. That makes this lead on Garz all the more significant. Let's get on that.'

The meeting has ended. I am with John, Jordan and Stevens, in Roman's office.

'If it isn't the dealers, it's probably the money guys, the bagmen,' opines John.

'I've got some fences who may know something. I am going to lean in on the dealers, though. It looks very much like a drug debt being collected. They would send out one of their enforcers for that. A low-level one, who can talk well. If it came to the hard stuff, they would send out one of the big boys or two. We know most of them well and the majority have done a stint or two,' Stevens informs us.

'Ok, let's spread it out. And we'll touch base end of each day unless it needs to be earlier,' John directs.

'Aye, will do,' Stevens concurs.

'I'm going to talk to Marty Danton. He usually has his eye to the ground,' I interject. I don't want to have Stevens operating on my turf if I can help it.

'No problem. He's all yours. I wouldn't interfere,' Stevens replies. He gives a courtesy nod as he leaves the office.

'Ok, Vilekar, you can contact Marty. Let's work our CIs as well. It's a priority now. The sooner we get to the bottom of this, the better. This is admittedly the best lead in front of us right now. And let's set up the drive-by check on Samuel.'

I must say I am disappointed that Nunes has that alibi. It looks solid. This is a guy who is capable of plotting a murder in a way that he gets away with it. Even with the irrefutable camera evidence, I can't help but think he's a good fit. But, right now, I need to work on real leads. We still have a killer roaming the streets.

Ashwin

I am sitting with my mom and dad and Ashwin, chugging a bit nervously on a cup of coffee from Starbucks. I think mom was a tad disappointed that I brought that along. She likes to share masala chai with me.

I must say Ashwin is looking in a far better mood than I had seen him previously.

'We have come to a compromise,' dad tells me.

I look at Ashwin.

'I am not dropping out of school. I'm gonna do my gaming alongside. I'm enrolling with a pro sports team and they will take me in their junior team to begin with. Then, after six months, I can try for the senior team that participates in tournaments. I talked to them couple of times and went to the center once. They thought I was pretty good,' Ashwin tells us.

'They will work with his school schedule. They usually have tournaments on the weekends, practices on weekdays, after school hours,' mom adds.

'Well, I'm not going to lie. This looks like a lot of work but I really am happy – and relieved – that you are going to stay in school,' I say to Ashwin. I cannot hide the smile on my face.

Ashwin smiles back. It's good to see my little brother smiling. It feels like a huge weight has been lifted from all of our shoulders.

'You ready to go?' I ask Ashwin.

'Yes,' he replies.

I am taking Ashwin to his team's training center, for his first official session. I volunteered to drive him. It gives me a chance to have the family chat. But an equally important reason is that I am curious to see the place for myself. I've always been curious about this world of gaming. Some of the most famous celebrities on social media are professional gamers. And from what I hear, they make millions, on par with professional athletes, actors and musicians.

This is a place around seven miles away. It's a complex of office buildings with modern architecture. We enter the building specified, using the enormous glass-and-steel doors. The gaming enterprise occupies the entire twelfth floor. When we approach the reception desk, the receptionist quickly checks Ash's identity and mine as well. We both go inside to a waiting room, one that has an array of coffee and snack machines, gratis.

Pretty soon, a young man, not more than twenty years of age, approaches Ash and asks him to accompany him inside. He turns to me.

'Hi, I'm Yuval. You are the elder sister, I take it?'

'Yes,' I reply.

'If you want to take a quick look inside, you're welcome to. But you will need to wait here. We only have team members in the training room.'

'How long do you think you will be?'

Yuval thinks for a moment.

'It's not going to be long, given it's Ash's first day. I would say half an hour, to get familiarized with the setup we have here. And then we will be giving him some documentation to go through regarding our team, competitions, rules and procedures. If you are pressed for time, we will make sure Ash is dropped off home.'

'That will be fine, I will wait,' I state.

'Ok.'

Yuval leads us both along a passageway and then opens a door at the end of it. I can scarcely believe my eyes. It's a huge room filled with television screens and what I learn are high-resolution monitors. There must be at least twelve of those. There are players for each of the monitors furiously making their moves. But despite it all, the room is silent, the silence broken only by the occasional whisper.

'They are all on headphones and microphones,' Ash whispers to me.

We leave the room, the occupants seemingly oblivious to our entrance or exit.

There are two more rooms almost identical in nature. Then we come to the training room, Ash's home for the next few months, until he graduates to the big rooms. This is a smaller place, less monitors and some trainees in conversation with their trainers. Yuval turns to Ash.

'I am going to leave you here with Chantal. She will go over the preliminary stuff with you and work on your schedule.'

Chantal is a young woman, probably the same age as Yuval. Ash takes up his seat and I retreat to the waiting, where I make myself a cup of coffee. I scroll through my emails and notifications. Our investigation of Tina Adams's homicide may not be over. But that hasn't stopped other homicides, kidnappings and other serious crimes from continuing at a pace that has only accelerated since the beginning of the pandemic. This may seem counterintuitive but is head-scratchingly real, nonetheless.

It's just over a half-hour when Ash comes into the waiting room.

'I'm done,' he says.

He is carrying some equipment and a bunch of papers. As we head out, he points to a room by the reception.

'I gotta keep some stuff in my new locker,' he says.

I follow him inside the room. He takes a key from his pocket and starts to look for the locker that is supposed to be his. I can't help but stare at the key.

'Can I look at that key?' I ask him.

'Sure,' he hands over the key.

I whip out my phone and open the photo of the key I had obtained from Tina's storage box. The two are similar. The only difference is shape of the key head.

When Ash is done, I walk over to the reception desk.

'Do you think this key will fit any of your lockers?' I ask the receptionist, showing her the photo on my phone.

She takes a look and then shakes her head slowly.

'Not here. But where I worked previously, we had keys similar to the one you got. That brand is not as popular as what we use here, but some places have that. I don't think they are in business anymore. Their compartments are a bit smaller,' she informs me, helpfully.

'Where was your previous place of work?'

She gives me the name of a similar firm in the west of the city.

'That's the biggest and oldest club around here,' she adds.

I drop Ash off but don't spend any more time. From what I saw, Ash is likely to enjoy his time as a gamer. Now, I'm off to the club that the receptionist mentioned.

But first, a stop by the evidence room to get the actual key. All I have right now is the photo on my phone. And I do not want to open someone else's locker by mistake and get sued. I takes me a half hour to sign in, get the key and sign out.

I reach the place just a few minutes before their closing time.

I flash my badge at the counter and ask for help.

'I have a key to a locker that could be part of our investigation. I was wondering if it belongs to a locker in your club.'

'Let me take a look.'

The man looks at it for a few seconds. Then he opens a ledger and scrolls down a couple of pages.

'It could be one of hours. I have a few lockers that have expired or come close to expiring and I can't get hold of the parties. If they don't renew within a week of expiry, we will remove the contents and store them in our lost and found.'

'You have a set of master keys, then? Maybe we can find a match.'

'Yes, we can,' he replies.

He goes in a comes back a short while later with a few keys.

'How come you don't have locker numbers on your keys?' I am curious.

'We have had thefts here in the past. It's easy to just open the locker when you have the number stamped. This is more painful but far more secure. And some of the stuff in the lockers can be pricey,' he informs me.

He is now matching the keys to the one I have. We finally have a match on the third key he tries.

'Who does it belong to?' I ask.

'The name here is Martha Gleason. I see that she was sent a notice a few days ago regarding renewal fees. Haven't heard back yet.'

'Have you ever met or talked to Ms. Gleason?'

'No. I haven't. But then, I have only worked here for about six months.'

I note down the name, phone number and address that is on file.

'Before I let you in, I gotta note down your id, badge and all that.'

'No problem. I'll give you a receipt for everything I take into my custody,' I reassure him.

'Ok.'

He leads me to the locker room and asks me to open the locker with the key in my possession. I slip in the key and turn it.

!!Open Sesame!!

I can scarcely believe my eyes. Miracles do happen. The material in the locker brings me down to earth with a thud. A bunch of folders with papers, journals and notepads. Also, a pair of headphones, a mouse and some packets containing chips.

'This stuff here could get you a couple of thousand, easy,' the man tells me.

I nod. I put everything in an evidence bag that I have brought along.

'I am taking all of this,' I tell him.

I make a detailed receipt on official KCPD stationary and hand it to him. He is satisfied.

Then, I head out to the precinct to examine the material.

At my desk, I carefully look through the papers. The journals and notepads don't have much to help, at least not at first glance.

I open the folder that contains a sheaf of papers. Going through them one by one, I notice a bank statement. The name on the statement is a commercial firm, GammaLambda Enterprises. Sounds like a fraternity. The name may sound like a boys club but the amounts are nothing to laugh at.

The statement is for just under a year. Over that time, more than three hundred thousand has been credited to the account and almost two-hundred-fifty thousand has been withdrawn, most of which seems to be by wire transfer.

The location of the bank is shown as Key West, Florida.

I set aside the papers after my examination and then call the number for Martha Gleason.

I get an automated reply that the number has been disconnected. Phone companies are quick to respond to unpaid bills. Sometimes faster than a subpoena.

I make a note to get to the bottom of the phone number and get Ms Gleason's contact information. But the priority is now the bank and the transactions that Kyle had spent so much effort on.

GammaLambda Enterprises

John and Jordan are sitting with me in a conference room.

'What do we know as yet about this company?' John asks.

'I accessed the CBP website for a search, using my security clearance. The company seems to be a shell company, owned by another firm. The origin looks to be the Bahamas, as far as I could trace. This account looks to be originating in Key West. That may be their local branch in the US,' I reply, with the limited information that I have managed to get so far.

'Ok, lets call the manager and get something more specific.'

I had sent an email to the manager earlier this morning. A generic one, saying we would need his help. He had asked me to call at this hour.

He picks up on the second ring.

'This is Detective Vilekar from the KCPD. I corresponded with you earlier today by email,' I recap our conversation.

'Yes, Detective. How can I help?'

I ask him for some information regarding the account I am interested in. There is a long silence on the other end.

'For any information on specific accounts, we will need a warrant and law enforcement credentials. I can't give out anything over the phone.'

He hangs up. We are all quiet for a while.

'I'll ask Legal to draw up a warrant, servable in Florida. Vilekar, you and Burns plan to get out there when that's ready. We'll ask Key West to make sure the manager or someone else is there to provide the information. I would say, take Hansie as well. He may need to use some of his skills, if necessary. I have a feeling we will need to be imaginative. These shell companies hide their tracks pretty well.'

There's a trip that I like to make. I've been to Key West a couple of times. What a great place. But right now, I feel a tinge of anxiety about what is behind this bank account. And another thought keeps popping up as well: am I (we) being led down the garden path here? The answer to that is too twisted to imagine.

'I am meeting Ms. Gleason this morning,' I inform my colleagues.

'What have we found out about her son?' John inquires.

'Her son's name was Kyle Juryk. He died of an overdose. The autopsy report says it was heroin laced with fentanyl. These types of deaths have become commonplace. There was no suspicion of foul play. The coroner returned a verdict of death by accidental poisoning,' Jordan replies.

'Each of these is a tragedy,' Elsworth observes.

Chapter XXV

Anjie

Ms. Gleason

Martha Gleason opens the door as I climb up the steps of the porch. The tragedy has added years to her age, and the fatigue that goes with it. Her eyes are kind but sad as she greets me.

'Detective Vilekar, I've been waiting for you,' she says.

I take a seat in the living/family room. The house is modest and well-kept. Martha offers me tea or coffee and I politely refuse both.

'Kyle was a genius. He could do anything if he put his mind to it,' Martha says, with a sigh.

'What did he like to do?'

'He was into computers, as you can imagine. And gaming. For so many years, he wanted to become a champion in that field. That was his passion.'

'When did he start? The gaming, that is?'

'He started at a very young age. In middle school. He joined the club when he was in high school. He was too young to sign for the locker, so I took it in my name instead. And he kept it in my name, saying I was his good luck charm.'

'I need to ask you; how did he get into drugs? I read the official report on his cause of death.'

'I don't really know. It just happened. When the pandemic shut down the club and the office where he used to work, that was life changing. Kyle had made a good amount of money from his professional gaming. I had no idea there was so much money involved. But then, he got addicted. I was trying to help him get back on track. The fentanyl took him. He was never into fentanyl, but it got him, nonetheless. You know, we have this war on drugs going on, seemingly forever. But, if they really wanted to save lives, they would make sure that the addicts were at least safe. From the deadly adulterated stuff and from overdosing. I can't believe we are letting this anarchy continue unchecked.'

The raw grief is overpowering.

'Ms. Gleason, did Kyle know anyone by the name of Tina Adams?'

'You mean the young woman who was found in the park? I think Kyle did know her. I never really met her. Kyle lived in his own apartment. But he did mention that he was working with a young woman named Tina. I never met her, but he did mention her name a few times.'

'Any chance they were romantically involved?'

'I am not sure. They could be but it seems unlikely. It's more likely she was a friend, someone he worked with.'

'It was also a business relationship, then?'

'It's possible. Kyle was quite active on bulletin boards. He used to do small jobs on the side. He worked on things like social media profiles, website design, even training for becoming a gamer. He loved his computers.'

Marty

Sometimes, the leads don't go your way. Correction: most of the time leads don't go your way. I have been in my office, perusing through emails, when I get a call

from Marty. It's not easy getting any information from Marty. There's always a quid pro quo. Mostly, it involves turning a blind eye to, or at least not looking too hard into, his latest activities. But, for the past some time, Marty hasn't been up to anything much. I pick up the call.

Half an hour later, I am in the parking area behind a small strip mall. Marty is keeping a watch, because, not two seconds after, he pulls up next to me, from the opposite side. We roll down our driver windows.

'Better have something useful,' I say to him.

'I think I have. Not 100% sure. There is a guy on one of the networks on the street. He goes by the name of Ragz. Now, sometimes, I heard he uses Garz, just to keep people guessing. You know, mix it up a little to make it less easy for the snitches. That's the best I got.'

'You have his real moniker?'

'It's Trent, Trent Weston. A badass, from what I hear.'

'You got an address for this guy?'

'That I don't. But I can keep my nose to the ground, if that's what you want.'

'That's what I want. This is a real priority. I want you to call me when you have a tip, day or night.'

Marty drives off, his dark window rolled up again. Man's careful and I can understand. The street is not a forgiving place.

Ragz

Trent Weston seems to have a bit of a record. Intimidation, assault, menacing. All pleaded down to misdemeanors. But someone with street cred, nonetheless. If anything, his star will only keep on rising. How it will end is anybody's guess.

It's quite possible that this guy Ragz may be the one who threatened Samuel. That seems to fit in well with his line of work.

It's well into the evening when Jordan stops by my desk.

'You still here?' she asks, the tone not very approving.

'Looking into this Ragz. He seems to be quite a character.'

'Well, I'm outta here. And, if you take my advice, you should, too!'

'I was thinking I will look at the gang affiliations of this guy for a bit.'

'Ok. But don't tell me if your love life falls by the wayside.'

Jordan flashes her smile as she leaves. There is more than a grain of truth in what she said. Spurred on her advice, I wrap up my research quickly.

The garage is quiet when I enter. There are some sounds coming in from the far side, where I know Rohan is working on his latest project.

I walk up to that corner and wait at a distance. Rohan is engrossed in his work. He hasn't even noticed me. I walk up and whisper,

'It's coming along nicely, looks like.'

He is startled, to say the least.

'Fair to say, your voice is the last I was expecting to hear,' he says, swooping in for a kiss.

'Giving in to my spontaneous vein,' I reply, laughing.

'You got anything planned for tonight?'

'No plan. That's why I'm here.'

'That's awesome. Give me a few minutes. I'll finish up in a jiffy. What say the Olive Garden?'

'That sounds great!'

I walk into the office. Rohan shares that with his other partners. It's a mechanics office, car parts and oil cans occupying a good portion of the space. I seat myself in one of the visitor chairs, a foldable metal type, which reminds me of those in our witness interview rooms.

Rohan is true to his word. He has changed from his overalls and there are no grease stains anymore either.

'Ready to go?' I ask.

'What's the rush? I thought we could spend some quality time here,' he replies, his eyes asking the question.

'Here?!! I thought this was business only!'

'No such rule on the books. Besides, I've got a nice sleeping bag and a blanket here. It's not the same as home but it's really comfy. Believe you me.'

'Wow. Ok.'

'Just reciprocating your spontaneity,' he grins.

'What cadence have you got in mind?'

'I thought Despacito worked well the last time.'

And so, there we were, in a garage, a single bulb the only source of light , surrounded by oil cans, auto parts and grease cloths.

Under the blanket, the warmth of our bodies together makes me oblivious to the cold, industrial ambience around us. Rohan is not to be hurried, starting with a slow kiss that seems to last forever. And I would hate to impose my impatient rhythm. So, I go with the flow, thankful, in my mind, that there is someone who wants to spend this time making love with me. When the time comes, I give myself in to the moment, wholeheartedly.

Jordan should start her own podcast!

The Olive Garden is busy, as usual, but we find a table-for-two. I think the strenuous activity has built an appetite in both of us. It's in the middle of the meal that I hear the phone ringing and see the called ID as the code word I use for Marty.

'Hey, I answer.'

'I have an address. He may be there now.'

I whip out my notebook and ballpoint.'

'Go ahead.'

I note down the address. Then I call John.

'Likely present,' I inform him, passing on my conversation with Marty.

'Ok. We don't have probable cause to go in. I'll station an unmarked car. If we find suspicious activity, we can search warrant on the basis of that. Keep your phone close. We could go in anytime.'

'Roger that.'

Rohan looks at me.

'That sounded serious.'

I just shrug.

'Well, I am really happy we got a moment to ourselves.'

'So am I,' I reply, sincerely.

We wrap up rather quickly. I decide to go to Rohan's place for the night. One of the reasons is that his house is closer to the address provided by Marty. It'll save me a few minutes. And besides, that was the plan, anyway.

It's one fifty in the morning when I get the call. The stress of anticipation has kept me up and I have been checking my phone every few minutes. I almost heave a sigh of relief when it finally rings.

'Vilekar, we have the search warrant. A male carrying two duffel bags was seeing entering the house. The officers clearly saw the outline of a gun as the suspect reached in to retrieve the duffel bags from the trunk. That was enough for the magistrate. The team is getting assembled. Note down the staging address.'

He gives me an address that is a couple of streets away from the address provided by Marty. I waste no time. Within three minutes, I am out of the apartment. Rohan is awake as well. He wishes me 'be safe' as I walk out.

At the staging point, I see three vehicles already there. John and Jordan are already in tactical gear. I see Stevens and another officer, name tag says Richards, who I assume to be from Vice, as well. They are just getting into their tactical gear. I quickly put on the Kevlar vest and grab the M16 from the boot.

'Follow my lead,' says John.

We drive up to the house in question. I can see lights on inside. Our car headlights are turned off. We park couple of houses down the block and move stealthily, in twos, the carbines at the ready.

'We'll cover the back,' says Stevens.

Stevens and Richards move to the back of the house, to cut off any escape attempt.

John, Jordan and I are at the front door. John knocks hard four times while announcing

'Open up, police.'

There seems to be a sound of rushing footsteps from the inside. One kick from John sends the door flying open and we step inside.

There is a sound of a door opening at the back of the house and shots ring out. Before I can blink my eyes, several shots are fired in unison. It sounds like multiple clips have been emptied. We sprint toward the back of the house. The back door is open and two individuals are lying on the grass. Stevens and Richards have taken cover behind a huge barbeque grill.

'Check out the upstairs,' John motions to Jordan and I.

We both quickly climb the steps to make sure there are no remaining threats. We move through the rooms and find none.

Outside, Stevens has already called for a rescue ambulance. One of the individuals is confirmed dead. The other is still breathing but injured. Richards is injured as well, having taken a bullet in the shoulder. Whether it was a direct hit or a ricochet, an analysis will determine.

'They had them at the ready. We ordered them to stop and they just opened fire,' Stevens explains, referring to the guns belonging to the suspects.

Richards has been rendered first aid. Luckily, the bleeding has stopped.

The ambulance arrives in just a couple of minutes, accompanied by what looks like a half dozen police vehicles, lights flashing.

A quick check of the identities reveals that the dead individual is Trent Weston aka Ragz or Garz. The injured person was not on our radar,but is now.

Dyson Thibodeaux

The sun is just about starting to come up. The hazy glow of dawn. The raid on Ragz's premises hasn't gone exactly as expected. That was more than an hour ago. Any operation resulting in loss of life is a major incident. IA will go through the whole thing, beginning to end, with a fine-tooth comb. Stevens and Richards have been assigned to desk duty pending an investigation. John, Jordan and I were let go after lengthy interviews.

For now, I am watching this apartment building, alongside Jordan, approximately six miles from where we served the search warrant. If it's going to happen, it will happen now. Maybe my theory is correct, maybe not.

I am waiting patiently, watching the comings and goings. Not too many at this hour. Then, I notice a hooded figure make their way into the building. From the clothing, and given the distance I am, it's not possible to identify this person. I have my camera with the telephoto lens. We are chugging on coffees to keep warm.

It's been just a few minutes, probably ten, when the hooded figure exits the building, the hoodie pulled low over the face. He is on his phone, gesticulating angrily. Jordan and I step out of the car. We approach this individual just before he steps onto the sidewalk.

'Hold it right there, and take off your hoodie,' I call out.

My hand is on my gun.

Slowly, the man takes off his hoodie. And Dyson Thibodeaux looks at each of us in turn.

'Kneel down and put your hands behind your back,' Jordan instructs.

Dyson does as asked, without resistance. Jordan slips on a pair of handcuffs and we put him in the back of the car.

Chapter XXVI

Anjie

Key West

Jordan, Hansie and I exit the airport and are met by a young woman, a detective from the local pd. Thanks to Florida and Missouri having reciprocal arrangements, Jordan and I have law enforcement credentials in Florida. This makes our job so much easier.

The bank is just opening when we enter. The manager is there, informed in advance. I hope he is more cooperative, now that we have a warrant in hand.

Luis Ortiz, the manager, has a nice office, nice chairs. He seems to be in a cooperative frame of mind.

'I am here to help. We always cooperate with law enforcement,' he informs us, expansively.

'That's good to hear. This account could be significant in our investigation. We need to get to the

bottom of who is behind all the money transfers. I've seen the transfer to the last few months. The sums are just enough to avoid SARs. But the sums are significant,' Jordan says to him.

Ortiz nods affirmatively. He hands us a sheaf of papers. Bank statements.

'These are for the past few years. If you look at it objectively, it's just like any other business with a lot of transactions. Nothing that would raise suspicion. And there are so-called shell companies operating for all sorts of reasons. The main reason is usually to hide ownership of assets. But that's far from illegal.'

The entries in the bank statements show entries of a similar type to the ones I retrieved from the locker.

'Do you have a name on this account?' I ask.

'You have to understand. This account is a subsidiary of an account in St. Kitt's. We don't necessarily check credentials about the person who presents the information. For the record, the name I have here is Peter McAuliffe.'

He gives me a sheet containing the personal information of McAuliffe. I am sure this will be a blind, doing nothing more than leading us down the garden path should we decide to pursue.

'The account is in St. Kitt's. Does it exist anymore?' I ask.

'I have no idea. It could or it may be closed down. We wouldn't maintain a check on that once we opened the account here. It did exist at the time, though.'

I shake my head. Hiding millions for the billionaires is so much easier than hiding a hundred is for the working folks. That's just the way the system is set up.

'Ok, here's what we are going to do. We need to get a real name matched with that account.'

The phone number does not work. The email address is the only option to contact the person. Hansie goes off to work with the tech staff of the bank. By mid-afternoon, we are all done.

I think this is the shortest visit to Key West I have undertaken.

Dyson

The witness room is where Dyson finds himself, again. But this time under very different circumstances.

'You got nothing on me,' he starts, when we are all settled.

'Perhaps you want your lawyer,' John suggests.

'I don't think I need one. What do you have on me anyway?'

'We know the apartment you visited. And we saw couple of holes in the wall. Guess you didn't find what you were looking for.'

'I don't know what you are talking about,' Dyson replies.

The fact that he didn't find the bags there is probably the best thing for him. That's his get out of jail free card.

We have a short conference to decide what to do with Dyson. He walks out whistling a tune I don't recognize.

'If Dyson didn't find whatever was stashed, we need to know who's got it,' John murmurs.

Setting a trap

Hansie has completed the setup for his communications monitoring. He brought all the equipment that would be required, anticipating this scenario.

The manager had sent out a letter by email to the address on file. It was terse and to the point:

''Dear Customer

We would like to inform you of a possible security breach of our banking systems. Your account is among the approximately fifteen hundred that could have been compromised. As a precaution we have locked and frozen the account to prevent any fraudulent transactions.

Please contact the branch within seven days of the receipt of this letter. If we do not hear from you within this period, the account may be permanently inactivated and you will need to open a new account.

Please have your personal information and banking pin ready with to enable us to verify your identity. The security of your financial assets is our utmost priority.

Best regards''

We hoped this would do the trick.

Two days after the arrangement was done, Hansie sends me a text:

It's happening.

It's just about the bank closing time. I rush over to his office. He is listening intently to the conversation, headphones on. This goes on for less than a minute.

Hansie takes off his headphones and looks at me.

'That was the incoming phone call to the bank. It's all recorded. Let me get that for you.'

I put on the headphones. Hansie double-clicks a file on his workstation and the conversation starts out. It's between the bank manager and an unknown make. The conversation is a series of question and answers, with the manager asking for personal details and the caller providing the information. At the end of the call, the manager states that he is satisfied that the information is correct and the account will be unfrozen.

I remove the headphones.

'Do you think the voice is real?' I ask Hansie.

'It may be altered with a voice modifier but it's not going to be AI generated. The Q&A nature of the conversation will make it very difficult to generate AI responses in real time.'

'Can you figure get down to the real voice? Assuming it's modified?'

'I can. I'll need to apply filters and algorithms to get as close as possible. AI may help me here. It's going to take time.'

'And the location?'

'The signal was bouncing off a lot of decoy towers. It's like a TOR browser for cell towers. That means the guy is cagey.'

'So you think it can be nailed down?'

'I think I will be able to get that but it may take a while to eliminate the phony signals.'

He calls me around half an hour later.

'The pinged tower shows the location of the caller a little south of Pleasant Hill. I will send you the map by email.'

The map shows the geographic location as a couple of city blocks, presumably the area covered by the cell tower.

By this time, it's too late to send a black and white to the location. Anyone operating from there will have long ago vanished.

Elsworth gets all hands on deck

'We need to get to this guy before he finds out it was a setup,' Elsworth says.

We have the whole team here. Myself, John and Jordan are in the front row, Stevens and Richards behind us. Richards has his arm in a sling, still recovering from the injury he sustained in the shooting.

I have just given a briefing of the information we have obtained from the bank. Hansie is still working on the voice identification.

'I wanted to get Vice in here too. The account could very well be a drug dealer's. We know this young man, Kyle, had a drug problem. He was great with computers and gaming. He could be a hacker as well. Bank systems aren't as secure as they tout them to be. In any case, we are treating this account as relevant to our investigation. We know the geographical area where the call came from. What we need is to put a face to the voice.'

'It could be drug dealers, could be anyone. We need to find them. The call didn't necessarily come from a house. It could be the street. Someone in a car. All we have right now is the vicinity. That's our starting point,' I point out.

'I'll get my team on it,' Stevens assures us.

'How's your shoulder? You can take a few days. I've already approved it if you were to ask,' Elsworth addresses Richards.

Richards has his right arm in a sling.

'I am fine. I can take the sling off if in an emergency. The doctors say it should take about a week to get it all a-ok. And you know, Lieutenant, I am certified ambidextrous as far as shooting is concerned.'

'Yes, I'm aware. That's why you're not on mandatory leave. How's the search for the voice id coming?'

'The voice was manipulated, so we need to get that filtered out as much as possible. Hansie is working with known databases. Hopefully, it's an ex-con whose voice print is stored. I'll update as soon as we get something.'

'Ok. Let's put this as our top priority. Get the whole lab on this. I would like to be briefed right away if anything turns up, night or day.'

We nod our Yes, ma'ams and leave the room.

I call Hansie from my office. He is still working on the voice id. There are a lot of samples to go through. While the FBI collects voice samples, it is by no means a complete database. There are state and local databases if there is no hit at the federal level.

'You can get your buddies to chip in. Elsworth has approved overtime for this,'

'Ok, that will help. Will call you stat if we get a hit.'

One would think two city blocks would not be that difficult to go through. But the fact is, we just can't kick in doors. The houses are not necessarily occupied by the owners. That's especially true for unsavory entrepreneurs aka criminals.

Elsworth stops by my office.

'We will do a canvass in the neighborhood tomorrow first thing. You can knock it off for the day.'

Can't say I am happy to leave things where they are. But a morning canvass makes more sense than going around knocking on people's doors at night. Jordan is in the building as well.

Hansie is still on his workstation when I get to his office.

'Want to grab a pizza, with me and Jordan?' I ask him.

'Sounds like a good idea. Give me a minute to wrap up.'

To say I'm famished is hardly an understatement. That goes for all three of us. After the pizza, I am still undecided what to do with the rest of my evening. After considering the options, I decide to go for a swim. The pool is open at this time and there are usually quite a few swimmers. There is something about being in the water that relaxes my mind, no matter how many things are weighing on it.

Dyson

Waking up, I feel like a million bucks. It's been a few days that I felt this way. I arrive early at the precinct, starting to scan the property records on the block that we are going to canvass. I'm about a quarter of the way through the records when I get the message about a victim of an overnight shooting. It's reported by a neighbor. Patrol cars are on the way.

The location of the scene is about ten miles away from where we were planning to canvass this morning.

The scene of a homicide has the same general look. Patrol cars, crime scene tape, forensics. When I reach the location, there are three patrol cars already on scene. The house is a small structure on a large lot.

I am the first detective to arrive. John is on his way. The officers on the scene have confirmed the death. Forensics and a recovery ambulance have been called in. I step inside the house. There are two uniformed officers who have already checked the house. There is no one in here besides the victim.

'No pulse. Vic's name is Dyson Thibodeaux,' says one of the officers to me.

I can confirm the identity on sight. I do my own check and confirm that he is indeed deceased. It's just a reflex action, maybe since my mother is a doctor and I've heard stories where individuals declared dead are found to be alive when examined at the morgue.

I quickly relay the information to my team and continue with examination of the scene. Dyson was shot at least twice. The police were called by a next-door neighbor who had taken his dog for a walk. He noticed the car door was ajar. The same neighbor had seen a white pickup emerge from the property early in the morning.

'I'm pretty much an insomniac. So, if I feel that the dog is ready, I go for a walk. It's usually nice and peaceful before the traffic starts building up.'

'Anything you noticed about the pickup?'

'It was a red pickup, sitting high. At least I think it was a red pickup. I saw it briefly in the streetlight. I couldn't see the license plate clearly enough. My house is too far back. I was looking out the kitchen window. Didn't think much of it. Then, when I took the dog for a walk, I noticed the car door was open and there didn't seem to be anyone around. I thought it better to get you guys to take a look at it.'

'When you say sitting high, do you mean it had a raised chassis?'

'Yeah, that's the type modified to be high off the ground. I hate coming across those on the road. They act like everyone should just make way for them.'

'Did you observe anyone, see who was inside the pickup?'

'All I saw was a figure in silhouette. The best I can guess, it was a man, just looking at the size, but I can't be hundred percent certain of that. I heard the pickup backfire a couple of times before I actually saw it.'

'A backfire? Like from the exhaust?'

'Yeah, you know, like a mobike sounds sometimes. The Harleys. Only, this was much milder, more distant.'

'How many of these did you hear?'

'I heard two from what I recall.'

That gets me thinking. The sounds he heard could well be gunshots, muffled by the fact they were fired inside the home.

'Thank you for your due diligence,' I say to him.

A red pickup is not much to go on. There probably are a few hundred within a couple miles radius. Still, that's something.

I'm recording the notes from the conversation when I see a message from Hansie, asking to call him urgently.

'I have a seventy percent match that the voice is Dyson's,' he informs me, sounding excited.

'Is that conclusive?'

'To take it to a court of law, I would need to have a match of around ninety-five percent. If you can get me the phone he called from, I can use the app to reverse engineer the distortion.'

'Ok, I will try my best.'

I take that in. This is more than likely a motive for the homicide. If it's Dyson on the call, then taking him out is an inside job.

Dyson's car was searched for weapons and explosives only at this point. Maybe the killer searched the car for the phone and left the door ajar while escaping.

The search teams and forensics are working inside the house.

'We need to look inside the car. Hansie needs the phone Dyson used,' I say to John.

Booby-trapped cars may not be that common, but it's happened on occasion. John and I begin our search for the phone. And anything else that may come up. The most obvious place for storing anything is the glove compartment. The phone isn't there. If Dyson kept it there, we're unlikely to ever see it again. I open the trunk. There is indeed a hidden compartment but that is empty. I push back the drivers seat to look under, just to be doubly sure. Nothing. When I try to do the same on the passenger side, I hear a slight clanging. It seems to give a little. Looking down, now with my flashlight, I see a small release latch on the seat support, obscured by the seat overhang. When I press on the latch, the seat is released, almost like in the fashion of a fighter jet seat ejector. What is revealed below is a small storage space, that now contains a phone (I hope it's the one I'm looking for) and a 25 caliber gun, one that will fit in the palm of your hand.

I bag both items, seal sign and hand them over to an uniformed officer. The phone will reach Hansie, while the gun will be tested for fingerprints, DNA, ballistics at the lab.

From the neighbor's conversation, I can surmise that Dyson was shot minutes before the neighbor observed the red pickup.

'I'll meet you at the station,' John says to me.

I nod as I get into my car. Elsworth is not going to be pleased with this situation. The direction I came in has now been blocked by patrol cars, an ambulance and forensics vehicles. Not to mention some news vehicles that have just arrived on the scene.

I swing my car to the other side of the street. The road is a bit longer this way. This region is a mix of a landscape, where the suburbs can be seen as transitioning into the countryside. Fields and farms mingle with groups of houses. A few minutes, maybe four or five miles, into the drive, I see an open field, of around ten acres, I would guess, that has small dunes and a track going in all kinds of different directions, ringed by a chain link fence. Towers with light arrays surround the field; no doubt for nighttime events. I have an idea what this is, even though it's deserted at the moment.

Reaching back to the office, I contact Hansie.

'I just got the phone, I'm trying to unlock it. May take some time before I can give an update,' he informs me.

'Let's hit a six with this,' I throw in a cricket metaphor.

I can hear his laugh as he hangs up.

I turn to Google maps on my workstation and open up the area that I just passed through. As expected, there are farms, fields and houses all over. The field with the hills and track is marked as a dirt bike circuit.

The next event is scheduled for later in the evening. It's promised as a summit of all dirt bikers in the region, with a purse in excess of twenty-five thousand for the winner. That answers that question. I continue scanning the map, now looking for the next thing I expect. Sure enough, around a mile and a half from the dirt bike track, there is a large single-story structure with a corresponding sized parking lot, called the Riders Club. In the satellite image, I can see some motorbikes and some vehicles in the parking lot.

By this time, John is back in the office. I walk over to him and share my findings and my suspicions. And the urgency to act right away.

'We can't get the warrant right now. It's all cooperation right now.'

I agree with him. It's a hunch but sometimes hunches come from intuition and are not to be easily dismissed.

And so, John and I find ourselves back in the same neighborhood we were not too long ago. But this time, our destination is the Riders Club.

As we approach, I see that there is a high wall surrounding the premises, with an iron gate that is locked. Old school. I ring the buzzer and someone comes on the speaker.

'Who is that?'

'KCPD,' I reply.

'Let's see some ID.'

I hold up my badge to a camera above the speaker. The gate moves shortly after and I drive in.

I see a man walking up to us. A young man wearing a biker's jacket and a cap with the peak turned back.

'I am Azar. How can I help you?'

I get out of the car and look around. There are dirt bikes, Harleys, trucks and sedans in the parking lot. But even among all of these, I can spot what I am looking for. A dark red pickup with a raised chassis.

I walk over to it, with John and Azar. It's a raised chassis, all right. I notice that the license plate has been caked over with mud. An old trick.

'Does that belong to the club?' John asks Azar.

'Yes, that is club property,' he answers.

'Can anyone take it out?'

'Only authorized members.'

'You have any camera surveillance?'

'No, we don't have cameras. They're just sitting ducks for government snooping.'

'You aren't afraid that someone would try to swipe something from here?'

'They'd have to be mighty lucky to get away with that. We usually have someone on the premises almost all the time and enough resources to call on.'

He probably refers to the armory they maintain. However, that's not my concern, at the moment.

'Did anyone take the pickup anytime last night?'

'Who wants to know?'

'KCPD,' I retort, rather impatiently.

'I don't know that I can supply that information.'

I look at John. He gives a subtle eye roll.

'Look here, Azar. This is a police investigation. If you are trying to hide relevant information, you could be in trouble. Trouble as in obstruction of justice,' I remind him.

Azar seems to be a bit unsure on how to proceed. Finally, he seems to come to a decision.

'Ok, look. Emilio was in the clubhouse late yesterday evening, finishing some paperwork. I can ask him.'

'Is he there now?'

'Yeah, he's sleeping in one of the bedrooms upstairs.'

'Ok, let's go wake him up.'

Azar goes off to fetch Emilio. He emerges about ten minutes later, with Emilio, who doesn't look too happy at being dragged out of bed.

I introduce myself and John.

'Emilio, did you see anyone borrowing the red pickup last night?' I ask, getting directly to the point.

'Like, what time?'

'Anytime, say between eight pm and seven am this morning?'

Emilio scratches his head.

'Ray took it out to the track last night. I saw him in the parking lot. He said he wanted to check out the track. There were some stretches that he thought might need some repairs.'

'Ray who?' I probe further, although I have a fairly good sense of what the answer is going to be.

'Ray Stevens, one of your guys. He's on the authorized list.'

'Did he arrive in his vehicle?'

'Yes, his Explorer. He left it here and picked it up after finishing with the pickup.'

I look at John. He nods. We need to act fast on this information. Right now it's all circumstantial but it's not looking good, either for Ray or for the department.

'What's this all about?' asks Emilio.

'Looking into a few things,' I non-answer.

We hurry back to the station. Elsworth is waiting. It's only myself, John and Jordan.

'Stevens is not locatable, surprise, surprise,' Elsworth informs us, with obvious irritation.

'He must've heard that we were at the club. Probably figures that the game is up,' John surmises.

'So, what made you think it could be Stevens?' Elsworth asks me.

'I wasn't sure. The other day, at the time we were raiding the house where Garz was hiding out, I heard Stevens say to Richards that he would rather be getting dirty on the track. Then, when I saw the dirt-bike track on the way back from the Thibodeaux crime scene, it kind of all came together.'

'I looks like he didn't want to risk being seen there in his own vehicle. This was a way to start the coverup before committing the crime,' Jordan adds.

'Well, he is in the wind. And no point using our police frequencies to track him. We'll need to form a task force and communicate on reserved channels,' Elsworth instructs.

Chapter XXVII

Anjie

The house on the island

I am on my workstation, trying to figure out where Stevens could have disappeared. I see a text from Hansie, asking me to come down to his office.

He is watching camera footage on his monitor when I walk in. it looks like a bank camera, with people interacting with tellers, an all too familiar sight.

'I am tracing all the transfers from the Key West account. I traced on to the island of St. Maarten. Then I asked for the customer information and maybe footage of when he or she was in the bank. Let me get that.'

Hansie opens another video clip on his monitor. It shows another bank setting. As it rolls, a man and a woman come in the foreground. The man is bearded, with dark glasses and a baseball cap on, but looks familiar. The woman looks to be in her mid to late twenties.

Hansie freezes the camera at that point.

'I did a facial recognition on the man. The disguise is good but I was able to do a point analysis. When I compared it to a photo of Stevens, it's a ninety-seven percent match. It's most certainly him. If I use AI, I get a ninety-nine-point-seven match.'

'How long ago was this?'

'Around a month and a half ago. The banks store quite a bit of footage. I could get more clips soon. Stevens is using an alias here. I used that alias to look for financial records on the island.'

'Using the DHS access?'

'Yep. I found that Stevens owns a villa on the island valued at approximately $7 million, all paid up.'

'Who is the lady?'

'Don't know yet. Not his wife, for sure. He is officially single.'

'Good work. We will need to build a strong case against him. If there is a weakness, he will find it.'

Hansie nods.

We are in John's office, with me on the whiteboard. It's a brainstorming session.

'It all seems to center on the bank account. If Stevens found out that Tina was tracking his payoffs, with the help of Kyle, he may have wanted to eliminate that threat. Even Kyle's death may need to be looked into,' John says.

'He kills Tina and thinks that's that. But then, you come up with the account information. That must have been a blow to him. He knew it was just a matter of time before we zeroed in on Dyson. So, Dyson's gotta go. And here we are.'

'I checked his whereabouts the night Tina was killed. He was off duty, no record of any communications. Of course, we had no need to check his alibi. He could be anywhere by now.'

'He won't be going abroad anytime soon. Or travelling by mass transit, for that matter. We have a bolo out at all airports, bus and train stations. I would say, his best bet is to lie low, in a safe place. Our task is to find that place. Let's track down all his past addresses. Also, contact his family, friends, club colleagues, anyone who may have spent time with him,' John lays out a course of action.

We get to work. I follow up on the searches I was doing earlier. Jordan and I scatter out to look for any leads that may provide a clue to Stevens' location.

The cabin in the woods

Three days after Stevens vanished in the ether, we receive a call from Johnson County, Nebraska. A posse of sheriff's deputies were following up on a call from a concerned citizen that led them to close in on a cabin in a wooded area. When there was no response from inside the cabin, the deputies forced the door open. Inside, they found Stevens, dead from a self-inflicted wound. He had been dead for some time, at least a day. 'Get over here, quick as you can. The flies are making it a sound like a buzzsaw,' the sheriff warns us.

Within the hour, I set off with John and Jordan. Johnson County is just over two hours away. The cabin is reachable by a dirt road, albeit one well defined. Jordan and I are seated in my car, with John following us in his. My desire to get there quickly means we have a bouncy ride. Insects are buzzing around and quite a few, unfortunately, end up on my windshield. I need to use my wipers to keep things clear.

It has taken us two and a half hours to get here. The cabin is surrounded by a phalanx of police cars, some marked, some unmarked. I can see the insignia of the Nebraska State Patrol on some of the cars positioned out front.

The scene inside is buzzing as well. The center of attention, of course, is Ray Stevens, sitting on a couch. His 9mm Beretta is on the couch beside him. It obviously slipped out of his hand after he had shot himself. The entry wound is visible just around the right temple. His glass of wine is on the table in front of him, still half finished. The TV that he is facing is now turned down to a barely audible hum.

In the kitchen, it's much neater than I expected. There're jars, containing tea, sugar, coffee; a flowerpot resting on a coaster, a set of knives set in a knife block. I see a bottle of anti-anxiety medication, prescribed to Stevens. Who knows what lies beneath the surface, I cannot help wondering. The last many times I saw Stevens, I couldn't have imagined he would be involved in homicides, ones he himself was investigating.

The forensics team is taking pictures of everything.

Hansie has followed us as well. He is taking pictures and notes, although the evidence is in the possession of the Nebraska folks.

A sigh of relief

Elsworth is, at the same time, angry, disappointed and relieved. This is the next morning, after our hasty visit to Johnson County.

'Can't believe we had someone like Stevens working alongside us, day in and day out. Now, we'll see how many of his cases are appealed. We're going to have all kinds of convicted felons out on the street again in a few days. There will be hell to pay,' she says, shaking her head.

I can see she is seething underneath.

'The cabin belonged to a family friend who passed away some time ago. Neighbors said they had seen Stevens there, not very frequently though,' I inform the group.

'At least we can close the case here,' Elsworth says.

The gunshot wound has been confirmed as self-inflicted, GSR found on Stevens' hand.

'Detective Vilekar, can you inform the Adams family about this. I know they are looking for closure. I don't know how far this will go.'

I nod a Yes. After the meeting. I am back in my office now. Making the call that we found the one responsible for the crime, albeit dead, should be easier than bearing the initial news of the murder. But, admitting that it is one of ours, I have to bear that shame.

Jordan is beside me, in my office. I call Jacob's number. There is no answer. I try a couple of times more and then dial Jennifer's cell. She picks up right away.

'I'm looking for Jacob,' I inform her, after identifying myself.

'He's out for a conference in Spain. He left around four days ago and he'll be back two days from now. He uses a different SIM in the EU. Is there anything I can help out with?'

I give her the information regarding Stevens. To say that Jennifer sounds shocked would be an understatement. However, she composes herself and commits to passing on the information to Jacob as quickly as she can.

There is nothing more to do here. The review of cases that Stevens worked on is now with the State Attorney. The press has been hounding the Chief and the brass, so much so that most of the higher-ups in the KCPD and the DA's office are using hidden entrances to get to and from their offices.

It's now the day after, although it feels like an age. I am sitting in a sandwich shop, nibbling on a grilled cheese sandwich, sipping on a green tea. The emails on my phone seem to be never-ending. Sometimes I wonder about the incessant capacity of humans to needlessly do things that they know will result in bad consequences. Needless being the key word.

Elsworth has closed the file. Most of the things Stevens did can be explained by one simple word: greed. A cardinal sin that most fall prey to.

There is this feeling I get when something significant is complete, over and not part of my life anymore. It's like my mind is a thousand miles away, not even noticing what is in front of me, like I am detached completely from my surroundings. It's happened to me when I graduated from high school and realized that that chapter in my life was done, it's happened when I broke up with my long term boyfriends, it's happened when I got shot and was recovering in the hospital and it's the same thing now. The sandwich is on the plate in front of me but my mind is far away.

I am aimlessly scanning my phone now, for the last forty-five minutes. I open the folder that Hansie has sent, with the pictures he took at the Stevens suicide scene. The photographs are all excellent, taken with any eye on detail, so much a part of Hansie and the reason I love working with him. There's the photos of Stevens, the wine glass in front of him, the gun by his side. Hansie even has a photo of the TV and the show going on at the time.

Then there's the kitchen. The counter, the flower pot, the neatly stacked utensils, some dishes on the dryer. Hansie even opened the pantry doors and kitchen cabinets for his photography. There I see the usual: coffee jars, dishes and cup, two sets of coaster neatly stacked in two piles of four and five, I notice that the design on the pile of five is the same as the one under the glass flowerpot, there are wine glasses, whisky glasses, a bottle of Blue Label scotch, red and white wines (most of the wines are AOC), spoons, forks. I glance over the photos and look away. Then I look at my sandwich, nibble on it and mull things over in my mind, nothing in particular, as I sip on the tea. It seems so inconsequential but I need to make sure. I look at the photos again. All so neat and tidy. And yet. I can't shake the feeling. Thinking what I am, I'm not sure I can just let it go.

I call John.

'It's too thin, Vilekar. I'm don't think we can reopen the case on that. And I'd advise you to lay off as well.'

That seems to be that. I can involve Jordan on this but I'm not going to. If I take any steps further, I'll own them completely.

A showdown

It's rather late now, after dinner time. I get up quickly and walk out to my car. I check my gun and make sure that my magazine is fully loaded. Then I make the drive out to where I think this will all end. End the way I expect or with my future in the KCPD in jeopardy.

I park just outside the edge of the premises. My lights are off. I think for a moment, take in the surroundings and then make the call.

'We need to come in tomorrow morning to take a look at a car on your premises,' I inform the lady who answers.

'Part of an ongoing investigation,' I answer when she asks me the reason why.

I note the time of the phone call. It is ten fifty pm. I get out of the car, I have my sneakers on, joggers and a running tee. I cannot make a move until I see movement.

I see someone with a flashlight moving in the dark, although I cannot clearly see their face. A door opens and a light comes on in one of the buildings. This is my cue. I may not have cause the search the premises but stopping possible destruction of evidence related to a homicide is reasonable cause to enter.

I jump over the iron gate and run alongside the driveway, keeping on the grass along the edge to avoid making a sound. I reach the door. There is a light at the far end of the building. I don't think the person has heard me. Very softly, I slip inside the barn, using the stacks of machinery as a shield.

I can see the collection of cars further down, a collection that I was impressed with when I laid my eyes on it for the first time. Under the light, a woman, wearing a waterproof jacket, pants and boots is working furiously with a water hose and bucket that I suspect contains water mixed with cleaning agents. She is cleaning one of the tires on the Landcruiser when I decide to step in.

'Jennifer, stop what you are doing and put your hands up where I can see them,' I issue the instructions brusquely.

'Detective!' Jennifer is taken by surprise.

She takes a moment to recover. Then her inner lawyer kicks in.

'You have a warrant?' she asks.

'Don't need one. You are committing a crime in plain sight.'

'What is that? I am just washing my car.'

'The one you used to get to Stevens's cabin. You are washing off all the evidence on the tires and the windshield.'

'You are trespassing. I can shoot you and walk away without even getting arrested,' Jennifer informs me in a dark monotone.

'Exigent circumstances. Just do as I instructed. We can sort everything out. It's my neck on the line if you are innocent,' I say, trying my best to reassure her.

I am still taking cover behind one of the SUVs, a Land Rover Defender. Jennifer complies with my direction and puts her hands up in the air. As I step out from behind the Defender, her right hand moves to her back.

'Don't do it,' I shout. But it's too late.

Jennifer has drawn her gun and is in the act of raising it. I have no choice but to shoot. I know I should aim for the greatest body mass, but I have trained my target just below her right shoulder. She has almost drawn level when I let go a single shot. The enclosed space of the barn causes a reverberation, like a concussion grenade going off. The forty-caliber should be enough to stop her. And sure enough, Jennifer is thrown back, the gun flying out of her hand. I quickly put on the handcuffs before attempting to stop the bleeding.

'You are under arrest for the attempted murder of a police officer. And I know you are responsible for the murders of both Tina Adams and Ray Stevens. We will prove it. Your luck's just run out.'

On my police radio, I call dispatch to send an ambulance and supervisor.

Jennifer is glaring at me. If looks could kill, my name would already be added to her list of victims.

'You fucking bitch! You were playing me all along,' Jennifer hisses. The injury is not life-threatening and she has no difficulty in directing her anger at me.

I nod slowly.

'I wasn't sure. I was hoping it wouldn't be what I was thinking.'

Even as we finish our little conversation, the ambulance shows up, along with police cars, their lights blazing and the sounds of sirens breaking the silence.

The paramedics are now taking Jennifer to hospital, under police escort. I am very relieved to see that her injuries are not serious.

One of the paramedic comes by to take a look at me. A check for any injury and then shining a light in my eyes for signs of shock. I'm given the all clear.

Jordan and John have arrived as well. John pulls me aside.

'I'm not going to mention our conversation. You took a big chance with this.'

'Thanks,' I mutter.

The adrenaline rush has started to subside. I feel like I hardly have any energy left. Even with the jacket, I am feeling a bit of a chill. Out of the corner of my eye, I see Elsworth step out of her official SUV. She has a word with John before scanning the scene. I am leaning against my vehicle. Elsworth walks over.

'Detective, I need you to go with IA [Internal Affairs]. You can have a union representative or a lawyer present. That's your right. In the meantime, you can keep your shield and gun. The initial assessment is that the shooting was justified. We have recovered the gun; it was registered to Jennifer. But you will be on desk duty as of now, until you are informed otherwise. I would advise you not to discuss this case with anyone until the investigation is complete.'

I nod. The procedures are designed to be rigorous. It's going to take time for it all to be resolved. It takes nearly five days before the report is published, with the finding that the shooting was justified. I can't help but feel relieved. I haven't said anything further to anybody about the events, not even Jordan.

Now, this morning, Elsworth has called the team into her office. It's myself, John and Jordan.

'Well, Detective Vilekar has been cleared in the shooting. Thankfully, it was not fatal. But, I am curious to hear what made you pursue Jennifer.

All eyes on me now. It feels a bit uncomfortable, especially when what I had was a strong gut instinct rather than solid proof.

'I've had a series of hunches about Jennifer. But things got serious when I found the bank account information in Kyle's locker. I found it hard to believe that Jennifer didn't know or hadn't heard of Kyle. Especially since Jennifer was responsible for the website for the drama club. And then, that led me to think about another thing I observed at Jennifer's home office, something I didn't fully register but later came to realize. Jennifer's office chair was very plush with a neck massager. But when I visited her home office, I noticed that the chair had a short back. Not very comfortable, especially for long periods of work. Then I noticed that it was very new, even the tag was not removed. It was only after I looked again at Jennifer's alibi that it dawned on me. Tina had a short back chair at her apartment as well.'

I pause for a second. Jordan looks at me questioningly.

'The alibi Jennifer gave us was bogus. We never doubted it because we figured she would never make it back to her place in time for her meeting given the timeline of the crime and the body dump in Colver Park. In fact, she conducted the meeting from Tina's apartment, after making sure that the background was identical to the one in her home office. And what was that? A flag of the two countries and a logo of the law firm. The color of the wall didn't matter; the whole thing was printed on fabric. Very convenient when Jennifer had to have different meetings with different groups of people. But also easy to replicate anywhere.'

I add my reasoning regarding Stevens's homicide.

'Jennifer knew she had to get rid of the dirt and insect marks on her vehicle. I managed to catch her in the act,' I add.

'My, you have a knack for this computer stuff. Must be your family background,' Jordan says to me, smiling.

I have to laugh. There must be something to that.

Elsworth asks me to stay back.

'The shooting was good. But your going all cowboy is not what I want. I want to be very clear about that. If it happens again, you might find yourself in a patrol car or worse. You get what I'm saying?'

I nod in the affirmative. There is no other choice.

'Yes,' I reply.

Ms. Gleason

It looks like we have spoken for the dead and done our part. Melinda Gleason, Juryks mom, has been traced. I would like to hand over her son's belongings, those that we don't need to keep as part of the evidence for the case against Jennifer. Melinda is now living an hours drive outside the city. The house is modest.

'Ms. Gleason?' I ask the lady who answers the knock on the door.

'Yes.'

'This is Detective Vilekar from the KCPD. We talked on the phone. I wanted to return your son's belongings.'

Melinda invites me inside the house. She insists on making a cup of tea. I can sense a sadness in her quietness. What an extraordinary burden to carry.

'I am sorry for your loss,' I say to her when she puts the tea in front of me.

'Thank you. I do appreciate the effort you took to come all the way here.'

'I wanted to let you know that your son was helpful in solving the terrible crime involving Ms. Adams.'

Melinda is looking at her tea. She takes a long sigh and then looks up.

'I am so happy to hear that. You know, Tina helped him and tried to get him to turn his life around. I suppose it is only fitting that Kyle did something for her in turn.'

'Were they friends then?'

'Yes, they were. Ever since Tina saw him in the line at the church soup kitchen, she stayed close to him. She was a true friend in need.'

I almost spill the tea. It's all I can do to keep my voice calm.

'The church soup kitchen, did you say?'

'Yes, that was a low point for Kyle. He fainted while waiting for his turn. Tina was extraordinarily kind.'

'Was she helping him with his addiction as well?'

'She was doing her best. She even talked to the dealer who was supplying his drugs. To no avail. She once walked in on Kyle while he was being threatened by the dealer. I think she was also trying to explore legal avenues to shut down the gangs doing all the dealing. It's too bad that it all came to nothing.'

I think my head is spinning as I thank Melinda and take her leave. I contact precinct and try to get the whereabouts of Samuel Bishop. The patrol car driveby has stopped a long time ago. Samuel is, and in reality always was, free as a bird. My next call is to Hansie, to get a rundown on all things Samuel. If he is who I assume he is, after talking to Melinda Gleason, then I would think he is capable of being in any corner of our planet, given the unknown fortune that Dyson Thibodeaux had been looking for when we confronted him.

I have now come to the address where Samuel is supposed to be residing, the safe location. I knock on the door. No response. The landlord opens the door and I step inside, hand on my Glock. But the apartment is completely empty. Not even a scrap of paper. The surfaces have been cleaned and I would bet whatever savings I have that there are no fingerprints either.

I head back to the precinct. My mind is racing over all the interaction I have had with Samuel Bishop. Anything that might give a clue about where he could be.

It's been a few minutes of my brooding when Hansie pops in.

'Tell me you got something useful,' I say, imploringly.

'If you mean a record, Samuel Bishop is clean as a whistle. But I did find something useful. Up until a year ago, Bishop lived above the liquor store when Luc Tyler was assassinated. I was able to find footage of him entering and exiting the premises.'

'How did you get that? A match, I mean?'

'I had the footage from the liquor store. That's for the last two years and a bit more. I had the footage of Samuel from his interview at the precinct. I was running a facial scan across the library and voila!'

Work life balance

The evening is nice and balmy. Say what you will but I don't think you can beat the weather out here. After that earful from Elsworth, I thought it better to keep a low profile and keep my head stuck in paperwork. I am about to leave for the day when I get a text from Rohan. I haven't seen him in a while. Too much on my mind to be good company. But now, he knows that the worst is behind me.

'Stop by the garage,' the text says.

I'll take him up on it. Last time things turned out rather well.

This time, when I enter the garage, Rohan is putting polish on an old Chevrolet Impala convertible, one of those antique types with the airplane-inspired design.

'I just finished this. Put a five-hundred-fifty hp engine with a brand-new exhaust. It will outrun any of your cars,' he tells me proudly.

I look at the car. It looks awesome. Sky blue and nickel and shining from the polish.

'Want to take a ride?' he asks.

'Only if you are going to keep within the speed limits,' I reply. There is no way I am going to give Elsworth more reason to put me on patrol duty.

The ride is remarkably smooth. When accelerating, the engine makes a roar like a racing stock car. It's what you would expect from a race car masquerading as a family sedan.

The wind in my hair makes my thoughts drift away from all of the last few days, letting me just enjoy the wonder that is nature. After a half hour, Rohan pulls into the parking lot of my favorite Italian restaurant. He turns to me.

'Want to eat in or get takeout to the garage?'

I know what he is thinking. Not very difficult to figure out. I take a moment and then look at him to reply.

Epilogue

Aruba. The sunsets are beautiful. So is the local cuisine. A blend of the local and accents of Continental. Is there a Dutch genre? I'm not quite sure.

I have been living here for the last three weeks. Every evening, I go to the casino, betting at the blackjack table. My winnings have been meager. In fact, I think I've lost money. I always use the private rooms that are discreetly tucked away in a corner. I like the atmosphere here. The clients are all high-end, the 'whales' as they are called. I am one of them.

For the past two years, I have been travelling from one coast to another. What was it before this? Ibiza? Marbella? So hard to remember. What I like about the whales is that they really enjoy the parties I throw. And my business has been going very well.

Tonight, has been a pretty normal night out. There is no party planned. Last call at three am. I call it a night.

'Good night, Mr. Cromwell,' the casino manager wishes me.

I bow my head slightly and step out. Out into the night. The valet brings me my Ferrari. It's a rental. But worth the price. I don't drink, if that's what you are wondering. It's a few minutes' drive to the hotel. The underground parking lot is quiet. But for some electrical work going on near the elevators. Hopefully, at least one of those is working.

I think I'll ask the electrician. Don't want to be stuck in that box.

I approach the guy and notice the door of the van opening. I'm right next to it. But it opens too quick for me to react. Three figures emerge. All in black, with ski masks. A hand jams down on my face and mouth and in a flash, I am hauled inside. Zipties are quickly slipped on my wrists. The electrician has wound up his job and is now inside the van as well. The driver has put the pedal to the floor and with a screeching of tires, we're away. Now we're speeding into the night. The road I had just traversed. I am unable to move. Around twenty minutes later, we come to a stop. The door opens and I am pulled out. Gruffly, if I may say so. I look around. This looks like a private airport. In fact, a Gulfstream is right next to where we are. The stairway has been pulled down. As I get to my feet, I see a woman walk down. She looks familiar, but I can't quite place her.

As she gets closer, I see a smile appear on her face.

'Samuel Bishop, we meet again,' she addresses me.

'You're the Kansas City detective,' I think aloud, almost reflexively.

'Detective Vilekar, at your service,' she replies.

'And if you are feeling hungry after this ordeal, don't worry. All your meals from now on are on us,' she adds, as I am hauled up the stairs.

The End
This was an Anjie Vilekar investigation

ALSO BY THE AUTHOR

Incident by the A1081

Detective Inspector William Roy of Scotland Yard investigates a double murder of a well-known barrister and his young daughter in the suburb of Barnet in London.

Roy is a Royal Navy and Marines veteran who has served in some of the most dangerous places during his military service. Yet, he finds that the foes he faces, here at home, are as vicious and ruthless as any he has encountered.

As he tries to re-establish his bond with his son and commit to his new-found romance, Roy finds himself moving inexorably closer to a dangerous confrontation with criminal networks and assassins who will eliminate any threat by any means necessary.

Sensual, spell-binding, edgy. This book is a must read for anyone who likes mysteries. A proper whodunit.